DESHAUN'S ROAD TO REDEMPTION

C.W. BURNETT

DESHAUN'S ROAD TO REDEMPTION

C.W. BURNETT

OAKLAND:
ALL I DO IS PEN PUBLISHING
2020

All I Do Is Pen Publishing LLC.
1603 Capitol Ave. Ste. #310
Cheyenne, Wy 82001
www.allidoispen.com

Copyright © 2020 Calvin Burnett

First printing: 2020

Cover design by: Jae Noirel

Graphic design and layout by: Hub Design

Edits by: Before You Publish-Book press

ISBN:979-8-5775-6159-8

To all the black men who dimmed their light to fit inside of a box they were born to stand on top of... This one's for you.

ACKNOWLEDGEMENTS

I would like to thank God for blessing me with the creativity to bring this novel to life; my intelligent, kind-hearted, beautiful daughters, Destiny and Summer, for not only being my reasons to keep striving for greatness, but for also giving me the concept of this book. I love you both more than life itself; my mother, Lynnette Robinson, for having my back through thick and thin; my siblings, Mia, Zsa Zsa, Jania, DT, Kia, Kevin, and Jalen, I love you all and pray for each and every one of you daily; my grandmother, Linda Meredith, for her prayers and wisdom; my children's mother, Dezzierea, for conquering the biggest battle of her life. You've become a better woman, mother, and co-parent because of it and I'm extremely proud of you; to all my aunts, uncles, cousins, nieces, nephews, good friends, and business associates— your support is greatly appreciated.

A QUICK WORD...

In order to travel the road to redemption, we must first understand the path that led us there. Whether self-inflicted or a victim of unavoidable circumstances, tracing the root of our pitfalls is the best way to dictate a productive future. Black Americans, men in particular, have been programmed to believe therapy is an ugly admission of being mentally weak. Therefore, we avoid it at all cost. Sadly, our group in particular, has endured more trauma than any other to ever grace this earth. Four-hundred years of oppression has led to many generations of severe mental anguish, which in return makes us ideal candidates for therapy.

Don't confuse the path to wellness as an easy one. It takes a supreme level of courage to leap into the realm of healing, and transparency is the ultimate act of humility, exposing many things. The good, the bad, and more frequently, the ugly will surface at a moment's notice. There will be days when you feel exhausted, overwhelmed, and defeated by the process.

When those days do occur, find motivation and inspiration that fuels your drive. It could be a child, parent, dream, goal, religion or even a significant other. In my case, it was all the above. I'd compromised each one of those aforementioned things on more than one occasion. In return, it cost me important relationships, my sense of self being, and eventually, my freedom.

Once I fully committed to the journey, the bleeding began to stop. Not the kind of blood that oozes from a wound, but the emotional kind that gushes internally, drenching every feeling that's needed to live a healthy lifestyle.

Therapy is not a cure-all. I repeat. Therapy is not a cure-all. Daily work needs to be done in order to persevere through life's many challenges. However, possessing the proper tools to diagnose the problems will give us more confidence and assurance to rectify issues as they present themselves.

Moral of the story is... Go and get help! Don't let society's stigma trick you into thinking it's beneath you. You owe it to yourself to be the best version of yourself.

Oh, and in case you didn't know—BLACK LIVES MATTER.

–C.W. Burnett

THE ARRAIGNMENT

"Nelson, get ready for court," shrieked a correctional officer through the distorted intercom system.

"Court?" I thought to myself as, I propped my head up from the thin pallet, posing as a mattress, shaking off the cobwebs of another long day with too much to drink—and way too much Xanax.

Over the past year, I'd become very familiar with the whole drunk tank process. A few hours in a holding cell, sleep the alcohol off a bit, sign a little citation, and bam, I'm back on my way—didn't even have to change into those filthy jail clothes.

This time was different. I was fully dressed in a pair of L.A. County Jail orange scrubs; and by the way the pants snuggly fit against my thighs, they had to be at least two sizes too small.

I yawned and stretched, trying my best to piece together how I'd actually gotten to that point.

The C.O. yelled my name again, only this time irritated and even louder, "Nelson, line up for court, now."

"Aye cuz, whoever da fuck Nelson is, better get his ass up," shouted a half sleep guy from the other side of the dorm.

"On the set, tho'. Let that guard yell one more time and I'm knockin' yo' ass out, on the 'hood," said another from a little closer.

After wiping the crust out of my eyes, I realized all thirty some odd pairs of eyes were surveying the room trying to figure out who Nelson was. Apparently, it was jail protocol to get up on the first court call, so the correctional officers didn't come fishing around, potentially discovering whatever illegal activities were going on at that time.

I'd never been in that position before. Therefore, I was completely naïve to the process. Nevertheless, I lunged from the top bunk, slid into my rubber, florescent orange slippers, and made my way to the door.

The dormitory door popped open. "Are you Deshaun Nelson?" asked a young, white deputy.

"Yeah," I responded in dismay.

"Damn, who kicked your ass?" he asked with a chuckle.

My jaw and eye were sore, but I honestly didn't know what he was talking about. Xanax, combined with Tequila, had a tendency of leaving me lost, searching for the answers to my prior actions. By the grimace on his face, I had to be busted up pretty badly.

"Show me your wristband."

I stretched my arm out, displaying the red band with my photo, full name, and eight-digit number on it.

"Red… That's Superior Court. Follow the yellow line down the hall."

"Superior?" I blurted while gently touching my tender jawline. I wasn't too familiar with jail lingo, but I knew superior court meant felony.

"That's what I said, right?" responded the scrawny, pale-faced youngster with a hint of aggression in his voice.

"What the fuck did I do?" I asked myself, trying hard to recall. But the pounding, dehydrating migraine blocked any little memory I might've had.

He escorted me to a holding cell where forty guys occupied a room meant to house twelve. An hour later, we were all shackled and packed into a blue transport bus.

I spent the next forty-five minutes staring at the floor, trying my best to process what could've possibly landed me here. The last thing I remembered was pulling into my ex-wife, Eve's apartment complex. I didn't even remember whether I'd gotten out of the car or not.

Before I knew it, the bus's doors swung open and we were unloaded into the courthouse building where another undersized holding cell awaited us. After being unshackled, I located a seat in the corner of the cell, balled into the fetal position, and listened closely for my name to be called.

"Nelson, you're up next," hollered the correctional officer before I could settle in.

Half the guys in the room jumped up, peaking behind the deputy to see which judge was presiding over the day's calendar.

"Man fuck, that's racist-ass Judge Bellingford," said a heavily tatted Mexican inmate.

A tall black guy towered over everybody and gave his two cents. "Blood, that's the bitch-ass judge who gave me eight years on my first felony case."

I was petrified entering the courtroom. The older deputy slapped the cuffs back on and ushered me to a wooden chair next to a court-appointed attorney.

His desk was fully covered with several stuffed manila folders. It wasn't hard to see that he was overwhelmed with a large caseload.

"Quick, what's your name?" he asked frantically.

"Deshaun Nelson."

He shuffled through the stack of folders and pulled one with my name on the tab. Without breaking focus from the paper he was studying, the slim white man with bad acne, a cheap suit, and receding hairline wiped his sweaty palm on his slacks and extended it. "I'm Baker

Norris. Nice to meet you, Deshaun." He briefly reviewed the paper and gave his spiel. "So, it says here you're being charged with assault two, burglary two, felony hit and run, fleeing or evading in the first degree, and driving under the influence. The DUI is usually a misdemeanor but it's being trumped up to a felony because it's your third..."

I was in complete shock as he read off the slew of charges.

Norris stared harder at whatever was written on the document. "Wow, third this year. The judge isn't going to be too happy about that. Anyway, this is an arraignment hearing, which is just a fancy way of saying first appearance. Judge Bellingford will ask to confirm your name, birthday, and address. After that, he'll set bail... I can see here that outside of the DUIs, you've never been in trouble. That should help when it comes to how much your bond will be set at and eventually how much prison time you'll end up with..."

"Whoa, wait a minute. Prison time?"

"Yes, these are some serious charges, Deshaun."

"How much time are you talkin' about?" I asked nervously, and then stood with my mouth opened as wide as my puffy jaw allowed.

The wrinkly, stone-faced, white-haired, Joe Biden looking judge called my name before Norris could respond. "Next on the docket is Deshaun Nelson."

"Hurry, hurry stand up. We'll talk about it later," whispered the dysfunctional public defender.

After repeating the questions my attorney had asked me, the judge glanced over a copy of the police report while wiping beads of sweat from his forehead. "Mr. Nelson, did your attorney have time to go over the police report with you?"

"No, Your Honor," I responded.

The judge poked out his tiny pale lips. "It says here that at approximately two-thirty a.m., you allegedly came to your ex-wife, Eve Nelson's place of residence, belligerently banging at the door. Once she opened it, you shoved her to the ground and forced your way in without permission. She also alleged that you dragged her into the apartment where her boyfriend blindsided you in her defense, knocking you unconscious, which would explain those knots on your face. Shortly after you gained consciousness, you rushed towards your vehicle, threatening to return with a gun. After speeding off recklessly, sideswiping several parked vehicles in the process, a patrolman responding to the nine-one-one call, flashed her lights in an attempt to pull you over. At that point you accelerated, eluding the patrolman for several blocks before spinning out into a ditch. After performing a breathalyzer test, it was determined that your BAC was three times the legal limit."

Bits and pieces of the story slowly came back as he read away. All I could do was lower my head in shame.

Judge Bellingford tossed the police report to the side before staring at me as if I were already guilty. "The court finds probable cause to charge you with the offenses mentioned in the complaint. Counsel, how does the defendant plead?"

"Not guilty," said Attorney Norris, from over my shoulder.

"The court is setting bail at one hundred thousand dollars. You're not to come within five hundred feet of Eve Nelson or Gary Clark. You have two weeks from the day you make bail to install an interlock device inside of your registered vehicle. Failure to comply with either of these mandates, will lead to bail revocation and an immediate return to custody."

"Thank you, Your Honor," said Attorney Norris.

"Hold on, counsel, I'm not done yet… Mr. Nelson's erratic behavior leads me to believe there may be a far more serious problem he's dealing with. In addition to the aforementioned stipulations, I'm ordering him to see a mental health therapist weekly for the duration of this case. If these allegations stand as charged, the outcome of his therapy will be heavily factored in at sentencing." The judge's eyes nearly pierced mine while loosening the collar of his robe. "Mr. Nelson, you have forty-eight hours from your release to schedule an appointment with Dr. Julissa Bishop. The court clerk is gathering all the information for you now. I strongly advise that you take the therapy sessions seriously. Otherwise, I'll make sure you strongly regret it. This hearing is adjourned."

And with the slam of a gavel, my fate was in his hands.

The public pretender patted me on the back and murmured, "I'll be in touch."

What the fuck did I get myself into? is what initially came to mind as the deputy returned me to the holding tank. The next thought was, *I gotta get the hell out of here*, as I watched the inmates tussle over the grotesque sack lunches the guards had thrown in the middle of the tank like dog food in a kennel full of angry pit-bulls.

I knew my sister Tiffany wouldn't have a problem covering the ten percent bond and collateral. She was well-off as a Marketing Coordinator for a respected black-owned pharmaceutical company in Charlotte and made six figures doing so. It'd come with a hefty tongue-lashing, but at this point, I deserved it. Tiffany always had my back no matter what. In fact, throughout my entire life she'd been my biggest supporter.

The whole therapy thing is what I was concerned about—outside of going to the pen, of course. Tiffany had been seeing a therapist since her sophomore year in college and often mentioned that I should give it a try. When my ex-wife suggested that we go after our marriage began to fall apart, my response was, "What the fuck do I look like telling people my business? Shit, to a stranger, at that."

Growing up in the 'hood taught me things like, "stay strong," "be solid," "man up," "keep your business out of the street," and "stand on your own two feet." It didn't matter how much you were hurting inside; black people didn't go unless it was punishment, or a check involved.

Either way, that shit was for the birds. I leaned on alcohol, cocaine, Xanax and occasionally, promethazine with codeine as my escape from reality. I must admit though, when the drugs wore off, it was right back to fighting feelings of failure and uncertainty. In all actuality, I was broken inside.

The trajectory of my life rapidly plummeted after Eve and I split. Imagine going from a college student with a load of potential to a thirty-two-year-old, borderline junkie, potentially on his way to the penitentiary—the irony.

Within a few hours, I was released. Tiffany's novel of a text message chewing me out was the first thing I saw as I powered on my cell phone. A simple 'thanks for bailing me out' had to suffice for the time being. I knew it was coming from a good place, but little sis' chastising had to wait until I at least ate and took a shower.

The peon-brained white bitch, Donna, I'd been finessing for the past two years, was waiting on me when I burst out of the building. Tiffany must've called and let her know what was going on. A few days prior, I'd taken Donna's rent money and blown it at the casino. No matter how bad I dogged her out, she was always willing to run to my rescue.

Her overdramatic ass started shaking and boo-hooing as soon as I jumped into the car. "O-M-G, babe, what happened to your face?"

"Bitch, don't ask me no more questions, drive off," I shot back, without a single regret.

As we made our way to the interstate, I looked over the papers from the court clerk. God knows I didn't want to see a therapist. But Judge Bellingford didn't really leave me with much of a choice. I saved the psychiatrist's number and hurled the papers out of the window. He gave me forty-eight hours to make an appointment. I intended on using every last second of it, too.

THERAPY SESSION #1

"Damn, it's hella nice in here," I said, while marveling the beautiful décor of the lobby. The mammoth skyscraper building was elegantly decorated with large paintings and foreign sculptures throughout the entire lower level.

As I rode the spacious Artisan elevator to the 19th floor, everything I'd been through the past week—month—year, flashed through my mind. My entire world as I knew it had crumbled right beneath me.

After exiting the elevator to the right, I took a deep breath before entering suite number *1933*. Once inside of the waiting room, I surveyed my surroundings. The low lighting, soothing nature sounds, combined with peace lily and bonsai plants gave the room a relaxing vibe. I took a seat in the nearest chair and skimmed through one of the many travel magazines neatly aligned on the coffee table.

Moments later, a forty-something-year-old, caramel complexion, brickhouse in heels, came ambulating towards me. My mind immediately shifted into horndog mode.

She reached out her hand. "Hello, you must be Mr. Nelson... I'm Dr. Julissa Bishop. Follow me."

Dr. Bishop wasn't just fine for her age—she was fine period. Her voluptuous body and million-dollar smile were definitely good reasons to adhere to her instructions. It wasn't even like she was dressed pro-vocatively. Her burnt orange silk blouse, tan and white plaid skirt, and nude-colored pumps met the business attire criteria. But her straight from the motherland, age-defying figure made it look sexier than what I was sure she intended.

I tried hard to think of who she reminded me of. My conclusion was the face of a seasoned Lisa Raye and the body of Ms. Parker from the original movie Friday. Regardless of which one she resembled the most, I would've given my left arm to beat her coochie out the frame just one good time.

My mannish mind had lust running all through it. I thought to myself, *If she really was about helping, she'd throw dat ass in a circle for a real one."*

I plopped onto the plush, cinnamon-colored sofa located in the back and positioned my left foot against the cozy armrest. You would've thought I owned the place.

"Well, I see you've made yourself right at home... Is this your first time seeing a therapist?"

"Yeah, it's my first time."

"Thanks for sharing that. Would you like anything before we get started?" Dr. Bishop pointed to a mini fridge with a basket full of treats on top of it. "There are danishes, granola bars, butterscotch, and peppermints on top, as well as bottled water inside."

I answered while glued to my phone, scrolling down my Instagram timeline. "I'll take some water."

Dr. Bishop reached into the small refrigerator and kindly brought me the cold beverage. "I'm going to need you to either mute or turn off your phone until the session is completed, please."

I hit the 'like' button on two more half-naked, insta models' pics before muting my iPhone 12.

Dr. Bishop positioned her black swivel chair facing me from a ten-foot distance. "Thank you, sir... Okay, let's start by getting to know one another a little bit. I'll go first. Once again, my name is Dr. Julissa Bishop. You can call me Dr. Bishop, Doc, or Julissa, whichever works best for you. I've been a psychiatrist and life coach for twenty-one years. I'm originally from Chicago, Illinois but I've been here in Los Angeles for a little over fifteen years. Don't let this fancy office fool you. I grew up in the projects and had to claw and climb for everything I've ever had. My passion in life is to help people heal—especially people that look like you and me. I also want you to know that anything you share with me will be one hundred percent confidential... Well, unless you plan on telling me you have dead bodies stacked in the basement somewhere..." Dr. Bishop grinned. "That's enough about me. Do you mind sharing a few things about yourself?"

I rudely directed my attention back to the phone and proceeded with my insta model lusting, "To be honest with you, I'm not really here for all that feeling sharing shit. I caught a case last week and for some reason, the judge ordered me to come do this whack-ass therapy until it's resolved... Can I just shoot you this hundred-dollar bill and have you print out something saying I was here?"

Dr. Bishop peered over her stylish, square-framed glasses before she tee-heed at my insolence. "Unfortunately, that isn't the way it works, this whack therapy you're referring to is how I feed my family. So, if you're not willing to participate during this process, I'm afraid that I won't be able to help you."

She rose from her seat and trotted towards the door. Once there, she grabbed the knob and turned a-round as if she was seeing me out.

The judge made it clear that messing this up would-n't be wise. As much as I didn't want to be there, I knew it was my only shot at avoiding penitentiary time—even though most people who knew me would say that's where I belonged.

I put the phone in my pocket. "All right. All right. All right... I'm Deshaun Nelson. I'm thirty-two years old. I moved to L.A. from Oakland when I was sixteen. I have two kids with my ex-wife and a possible baby by a bitch that never should've been pregnant in the first place. I lost my house, my job, and everything else I ever gave a fuck about because of it. I just committed a gang of felonies, including my third DUI, and I'm pretty sure I'll be going to prison soon... Anything else you need to know?"

Dr. Bishop returned to her seat. "Thanks for sharing that... I'm not a fan of the profane language, but I'm willing to accept it as long as you agree to fully engage throughout the duration of our time together."

I made one last plea, "On some real shit though, Doc, can I just give you two-hundred then? All I need is a printout saying that I was here."

"Sir, please stop insulting my integrity. You couldn't bribe me with a million unmarked dollars in a bulletproof briefcase... Besides, didn't you just say that you lost your house, job, and might be going to jail soon? Sounds like you could put that two hundred to better use... Now, can we please continue?"

I felt slightly played but I let it ride. Dr. Bishop clearly had a feisty side.

She adjusted her knee length pencil skirt, crossed her legs, and flipped open the cover of a small, green notepad. "If you don't mind me asking, what happened to your face?"

I blew steam from my nose while reminiscing about that dreadful night. "I got jumped by my ex-wife and her new boyfriend before I got arrested."

She winced as if she could literally feel my pain. "Is it okay if we talk about that for a second?"

"See, I told you I wasn't trying to get into all that kind of shit."

Dr. Bishop tapped the pen against the pad and tilted backwards, "Mr. Nelson, I thought I made myself clear."

The fact that I was able to remember everything, once my high came down, really pissed me off. I most definitely didn't want to relive that embarrassing night. But I also didn't want to risk her prematurely ending the session.

"Are you sure whatever I tell you won't leave this room?"

"As a therapist, I made a vow to protect the confidentiality with all of my patients—even the ones who're in trouble. The only thing I'm obligated to share with the courts is a report on the day of your sentencing giving a recommendation of whether I think rehab would be a better option than prison."

I didn't know if she was telling the truth or not, but rehab sounded way better than prison. I paused for a second to gather my thoughts. "All right, so this is what happened."

●●●

Last Friday night, I met a few of the guys at a pool hall in Torrance called Mr. Lucky's. I'd been up partying since early that morning, so I was already fucked up when I got there. After several more shots of tequila, I knew that it was time to call it quits. When I got in the car, my head started spinning. I thought about sleeping it off in the backseat of my truck, but Eve's place was only a few blocks away. I figured I'd just slide over there to sober up. I knocked on the door, but she wasn't answering. I knew she was in there because her car was parked outside. And shit, where else would she be at two-thirty in the morning?

The fact that she was ignoring me made me angry. I banged, kicked, and yelled out a few bitches and hoes, until she finally opened the door. She squeezed through the door as if she were hiding something. When I tried to go inside, she put out her arms, blocking my pathway. I muscled my way in, accidentally knocking her to the ground. I barely shoved her, so it wasn't any reason for her to be stretched out and groaning the way she was.

Once inside, I went into the kitchen to get something to eat. By that time, Eve's dramatic ass was peeling herself off the floor as if Hulk Hogan had body slammed her. I glanced over to tell her to get up, then out of my peripheral, I see this blur rushing towards me. Next thing I know, I'm being fired on from every direction. Mind you, I'm drunk and high, so it really wasn't much I could do after the coward sucker punched me. I ended up losing consciousness before waking up to Eve dousing a pot of cold water in my face. When I got up, her bitch-ass boy-friend was standing in the hallway mean-mugging with his shirt off. The pussy was lucky I was loaded or else I would've beaten his ass right then and there.

I rushed down to my Tahoe and raced out of the complex. I couldn't believe Eve let that buff nerd sneak me like that. I flipped down the visor mirror to see how much damage had been done. Not only did I see my face drenched in blood, I saw red and blue police lights flashing behind me. It was a weak-ass lady officer at that. She must've been parked right outside of the exit gate. I tried to shake her for a few blocks, but she was already glued to me. That's what happened... to my face and how I caught the case.

● ● ●

"Sounds like one hell of a night, Mr. Nelson. Had you and Eve's boyfriend had any encounters prior to that?"

"Nah, that was my first time seeing him. The kids had already met him, so I did know about him."

"Speaking of the kids... Where were they when all of this was taking place?"

"At my momma's house."

"Well, that's good to know. Children should never have to witness violence of any sort, let alone domestically amongst their parents... So, you mentioned that they'd previously met the boyfriend. How'd that make you feel?"

"I wasn't feelin' that shit at all. Out of respect, she

should've checked with me first."

"Would you have checked with her first if the shoe was on the other foot?"

I was caught off guard by her question and inadvertently stuttered before responding. "It—it's different for a man though. I'm a father and a protector. I need to know who's going to be around my kids at all times."

"Pardon me, but don't you see the double standard in that statement?"

"Double standards exist for a reason. Some favor men, some don't. This just happens to be one that does," I said, while staring her dead in the eyes without flinching.

"Tuh, I heard that." Dr. Bishop's comeback had sarcasm written all over it. "How long have you two been divorced?"

"Almost a year now."

"How long were you married?"

"Ten."

Dr. Bishop smiled. "And that union produced two wonderful children... Isn't that a blessing?"

"Yeah, Deshaun Jr. and Denisha. My two reasons for breathing."

Her eyes twinkled after my statement. "Children are such an amazing blessing. They always find a way to bring out the best in situations, don't they?"

"Well, hold up now... Not necessarily," I said, while shaking my head and waving my hand.

Dr. Bishop's shoulders hunched, and eyebrows lifted. "Can you explain why you disagree?"

"When Eve got pregnant with Denisha, our marriage took a turn for the worse. Don't get me wrong, that's my little princess... But her being conceived wasn't a part of the plan."

"It's interesting that you used the term 'turn for the worse'. Were things good between you two before she got pregnant with your daughter?"

I couldn't fight back the grin. "Honestly, things were great."

Dr. Bishop jotted for the first time into the notepad she was holding. "Perfect, let's start there. I like to encourage my patients to fill the room with positive energy before we dig into all the negative... Trust me, there'll be plenty of time to discuss the bad stuff." She flashed her adorable dimples and winked, causing me to blush a little.

I took a swig from my water bottle. "Do you want me to start from the very beginning?"

"Yes, please."

●●●

Eve and I met in our freshmen year of college. We had a creative writing class together. It was love at first sight—for me at least. Not so much for her. In reality, Eve shut me down the entire semester. Every day I'd offer to buy her a burger and fries from Habit Burger, and each time she declined. I don't know if it was persistence or ignorance, but I never stopped trying. One day, to my surprise, she finally accepted. From that day forward, we were inseparable.

At the end of our junior year, she got pregnant with Deshaun Jr. I was so excited to be a father because my dad wasn't in my life growing up. So, the opportunity to raise a son felt amazing.

As an early graduation gift, Eve's parents paid for us to have a small wedding. They were very religious and didn't want Deshaun Jr. being born out of wedlock. Shortly after, I temporarily quit school and got a job at my grandfather's body shop. We managed to move off campus into a tiny apartment located in a rough part of town called Baldwin Village, on Coco Avenue. It wasn't much, but it was ours.

I worked so much during that time. I'd get home, take a shower, shove some food in my mouth, sneak a couple hours of sleep, and go right back to work. It didn't matter though. I was willing to do whatever it took to make sure my family had what we needed.

On June 7, 2009, my baby boy was born. It was literally the happiest day of my life. Watching a tiny version of me being brought into this world gave me so much joy. Eve had given me the son I'd always prayed for.

She graduated a few months later. To be honest, it was a bittersweet moment for me. Of course, I was proud to see her walk across the stage. Especially after witnessing her balance an infant and online classes, in order to complete the necessary final credits. Another part of me was envious it wasn't me holding that degree. The dream of becoming a filmmaker had gotten me through some rough times growing up. However, I knew that my time would come. It was just a matter of being patient.

Everything was going according to plan. Eve got a management position at the bank and was bringing in good money. With our salaries combined, we eventually saved enough for a down payment on a home. We were on cloud nine. In just a little over two years, we'd managed to fulfill most of our short-term goals. The only goal left was me obtaining my degree. UCLA had a highly touted film program I'd always wanted to attend. By the grace of God, I was accepted. Opening that letter and seeing my name next to UCLA's letterhead was almost as gratifying as the day Deshaun Jr. was born. All the grief and sorrow of my childhood didn't matter anymore. I was creating a whole new narrative as an adult.

Eve and I both worked extra hours in order to prepare for me going back to school full time. Her mom helped out a lot with the baby so, it made it easier for us to pick up extra shifts. I was super excited to get started.

And then, it happened. On February 18, 2012, a week before the start of the spring semester, Eve surprised me with a pregnancy test dipstick. She even put a little bow on top of it. The two lines indicated that we would be expecting another child. I immediately felt betrayed.

●●●

"Let me stop you right there for a second," said a fully engaged Dr. Bishop. "That's a very bold description of your feelings during that moment. Do you honestly think she intentionally got pregnant just to stop your plan?"

"For years I did, but in hindsight... No," I said, while rubbing my hands together.

"Well, had she given you any prior indication for you to draw that conclusion?"

"Eve wanted a lot of kids... I didn't. Every time she brought up the idea, I'd shut it down. So, when she mysteriously popped up pregnant again, I instantly felt like it was a trap."

"A trap? Correct me if I'm wrong, but you speak as if you didn't trust your wife."

"I don't trust anybody. Never have... And probably never will."

Dr. Bishop squinted. "Not even your parents?"

"Definitely— not."

"Very interesting..." Dr. Bishop scribbled in her pad before changing the subject. "So, Eve surprised you with the positive pregnancy test. Tell me what happened next?"

● ● ●

So many things raced through my mind. Happiness wasn't one of them. My first thought was, *How are you pregnant if you're wearing the patch?* Next, I thought, *How are we going to afford another baby if I'm going to school full time?* Then it hit me. School would be the only sacrifice in the equation. The only person whose life would change was mine.

Eve had her degree. Meanwhile, I was slaving at the body shop, working twelve-hour days, trying to be the opposite of the no-good men I'd watched growing up. The only thing that kept me sane was the dream of completing film school. And here she was snatching it away from me again, with another baby I didn't ask for.

I was so furious that before I knew it, I'd palmed the side of her face. That was my first time ever putting my hands on a woman. I'd never even raised my voice at Eve prior to that. I'd witnessed so much domestic violence growing up that I swore to never partake in it. But for some reason, my natural instinct was to smack her. She dropped to one knee and held the side of her face. The helpless, confused reaction she had reminded me of a look I'd given on multiple occasions as a child. I knew firsthand what it felt like to be abused. Sadly enough, it felt empowering being on the other side of it. In my mind, she deserved it.

From that moment forward, shit spiraled out of control. I started staying out late and drinking more than usual. In the beginning, it was just me shooting pool, hanging with the fellas. That quickly turned into me entertaining other women.

Out of the few women I'd been seeing, Trina Davis, was the one who stood above the rest. She and Eve were complete opposites. Eve was tall, dark, and athletic. Trina was short, light-skinned, and thick. Eve was classy, conservative, and soft-spoken. Trina was ratchet, loud, and sassy. Eve was into religion, education, and things of substance. Trina only cared about clothes, purses, and getting high. I needed what Eve offered at home, but I desired what Trina had to give everywhere else.

You'd think that sex would be the last thing on my mind after how poorly I responded to Eve's pregnancy bombshell. Nonetheless, Trina and I got busy every chance we could. In the car, at the park, daytime, nighttime it didn't matter. Her juicy thighs, small waist, and tattoos in all the right places turned me on without a moment's notice. She'd even invite other ladies to join in from time to time. On any given night it'd be two or three other females in the bed with us.

Before that, Eve's and my sex life was nonexistent. Between work and the baby, we never had the time or energy to make love. At that point, sex had been limited to pre-planned, missionary-style quickies while Deshaun Jr. took naps. That was even more reason why I was shocked when she sprung the pregnancy news on me.

I began to risk it all in order to see Trina more often. What started off as a weekend fling, became an everyday affair. Eve had suspicions that something was going on, but I didn't care. Nothing was going to stop me from seeing Trina.

One night, Trina asked me to hog-tie, spit in her mouth, then gag her. It was such a wild, freaky, off-the-wall request that I had to try it. My mind was blown by the feeling of watching her bent like a pretzel. Eventually, that led to me snorting lines of coke and ecstasy off of her asscheeks and licking promethazine with codeine from her titties. Needless to say, I became addicted to all three drugs. Well, four if you include Trina. My body no longer wanted her, it craved her. I felt so alive and free when we were together. Trina was my ultimate escape from reality.

About six months into my shenanigans, Eve finally decided to confront me. Apparently, a condom and coke baggy had fallen out of my pants pocket while she was doing laundry. I fessed up to the coke but diligently denied having an affair. I knew admitting that I was falling for another woman would break her. Although I was unhappy with the timing of the pregnancy, Eve was still my wife. I cared about her well-being. She recommended that we go to marriage counseling. I agreed only to delay her complaining. It wasn't any use. I was too far gone already. Trina and the drugs had a lock on me.

●●●

Dr. Bishop's lips puckered as she side-eyed me. "Sounds like you and Ms. Trina really hit it off there, huh?"

I tried to downplay it, but I was sure the sparkle in

my eye told a different story. "I guess you could say that."

"Mm hmm... It seemed as if things were going really well between Eve and yourself in the beginning... Actually, all the way up until the 'gift' she presented you with. I guess my question is... Was there a prior episode that might've triggered your urge to unleash, so to speak?"

"I mean... We had our little ups and downs like every other couple, but nothing really worth mentioning. If anything, I'd say the non-stop grind of working towards buying that house, combined with the disappointment from not being able to finish school, is what ultimately did it for me."

Dr. Bishop's glower led me to believe she wasn't too satisfied with that answer. "You mentioned that Trina was the total opposite of Eve. If you both were so happy before the second pregnancy, why'd you feel the need to find someone so different? Better yet, why even find someone else at all? You didn't think you and her could've worked things out, seeing that there wasn't any real drama beforehand?"

"I never intended to cheat. Everything just happened so fast... Yeah, things were good between us, and I'm sure we could've put whatever issues we had behind us. But being with Trina was like living out a fantasy. Before I knew it, I was caught up in her spell."

Dr. Bishop grabbed a box of Kleenex from her desk, removed one, and cleaned her glasses with it. She fidgeted in her seat and placed her glasses back on the tip of her nose. "Mr. Nelson, you might not like what I'm about to say, but I'm going to say it anyway, because you really need to hear it. So far, I've heard you place blame on two women for the decisions you made as a sound-minded adult. First, it was Eve's fault why you decided to go out and be a busybody. You even went as far as to say she deserved being physically abused while carrying your child. Then you accused Trina for your own extramarital behavior, implying that she casted a spell on you, and strung you out on drugs." She ran her fingers through her hair and paused. "I'm not a betting woman by any means. But if I was, I'd bet my last that your issues with women span far deeper than the two ladies mentioned... How was you and your mother's relationship growing up?"

My body tensed up as soon as the question left her mouth. The scowl on my face indicated exactly what Dr. Bishop was fishing for. Things between Momma and me were complicated and even being asked about it bothered me. "Not all that good. But look... I really ain't tryna get into all that."

Dr. Bishop documented my answer with a smirk on her face. I knew then the same topic would resurface later.

"As you wish, Mr. Nelson." She flicked her wrist, revealing a shiny gold wristwatch. "That pretty much concludes our time for today. I must say, you did well."

"Thanks," I responded, while snatching a few snacks from the top of the fridge as I made a beeline for the door.

"You're welcome... Be sure to schedule next week's appointment with my receptionist on your way out. Until then, have a wonderful week."

The first session wasn't bad at all. 'A few more of these and I should be all good come judgement day,' is what I said to myself while waiting for the cute, young receptionist to book my next appointment.

"Do you prefer mornings or afternoons, Mr. Nelson?" asked the dark-skinned Nubian Queen.

"I prefer whatever time you plan on being here, baby," I shot back before licking my lips.

The slim, dreadlock-wearing lady rolled her eyes and wrote a random date and time on a card. "Your appointment is next Tuesday at ten a.m.," she said while handing it to me.

I made sure to graze her hand before taking a glimpse at it. "Damn, yo' phone number don't come wit' it?"

"Have a nice day, sir," she said in a dry tone.

"Same to you, sexy... Next time I'mma need that number tho'," I heckled while exiting the office.

THERAPY SESSION #2

As I moseyed into the lobby the following Tuesday morning, the first person I spotted was the pretty, petite receptionist. She was at her desk filing paperwork when I strolled towards her. I waved in her direction. She purposely ducked her head, doing her best to avoid me. I chuckled as I slid into Dr. Bishop's office.

She was already in her chair ready to rock and roll. "Good morning, Mr. Nelson. It's great to see you again."

"Top of the morning, Doc," I replied while picking through the goodies basket.

"How was your week?" she asked with a huge grin.

"It was a'ight, I guess."

"Just a'ight?" she asked, mocking my tone.

"Yep. Same ol' same ol'. Nothing too major."

"Okay, Mr. Same ol' same ol'. Is there anything you'd like to discuss before we get started?"

"Nah, I'm good. Go ahead," I said while munching on the danish I'd snagged from the treat section.

Dr. Bishop rolled back the cover of the notepad. "If you don't mind, I'd like you to finish telling me what happened after your daughter was born. Did any of your reservations change?"

•••

On November 23, 2012, my baby girl, Denisha, was delivered. She looked just like me. Every negative feeling I had went away when I stared into her gorgeous brown eyes. My issue was never with the baby. It was always with Eve and the timing of the pregnancy.

She and I didn't discuss my infidelities after the baby was born. We basically swept it all under the rug. I think she was just happy to see me accepting Denisha.

Things even simmered down between Trina and me. I explained to her that I wouldn't be able to see her as often. I still would make it a point to link up with her a couple times a month just to let off some steam. We'd go to a bar, have drinks, and end up at Motel 6 for a couple hours or so. Trina didn't have her own apartment anymore. So, getting a room was our only option. Sometimes, I'd tell Eve I was making a quick store run and meet Trina around the corner for a quickie in the car.

This pattern went on for a few years. Every now and then, Eve would go through my phone, see text messages from Trina, and make sly remarks. She knew better than to get out of line though.

I was still getting high, too. I'd dip off to snort a line or sip some lean whenever possible. Everything was going pretty smooth if you ask me. Eve knew what I was doing the whole time. Why she never said anything, I'm not sure. I couldn't have cared less how the fuck she felt during that time anyway. Honestly, as long as the mortgage and bills were paid, she really couldn't say shit. The only reason I was being discreet about the drugs was for the kids. I grew up watching people in my family get high and drunk, so I never wanted my kids to see me doing it.

Eventually, Trina had gotten her life together. She went to rehab and completely let go of the drugs. I gave her the first, last, and deposit on an apartment after she completed treatment. Shortly after, she enrolled into nursing school. A year had passed and she was still on the right track.

Everything was good until she started asking for too much. First, the bitch wanted me to stop getting high. She'd always complain about it being a trigger for her. I was like "Fuck no. Just because yo' ass all clean and sober, don't mean I gotta be. Plus, yo' ass is the one who got me hooked in the first place." After that, she made an issue about us not spending enough time together. I'm thinking to myself like, *after all these years, bitch now you wanna complain about time?* On top of that, she knew what it was from the beginning. Being a side piece meant falling back and playing her position. Whatever time I gave her was the time her ungrateful ass was gettin'... Simple as that. The final straw was when she started talking about us having a baby together.

Before she could even finish her sentence, I reached out and choked the shit out of her. "Eve is my mothafuckin' wife, bitch. If I'm going to have any more kids, it's gon' be by her, not yo' ass."

Trina hadn't seen that side of me before. I could tell she was scared. I let go of her neck, hoping that I'd gotten my point across. Man, was I so mothafuckin' wrong.

●●●

Dr. Bishop scratched her head. "How many years were you living this double life?"

"All together... About six."

"Did you ever feel any remorse?"

"Remorse? For what? Nobody ever had remorse for the shit they did to me."

"So, at no point during those six years did you feel bad about what you were doing?"

"A little bit... But like I said before... Eve was happy to have me around the house and Trina was good until she stopped getting high. Everybody was satisfied until then."

"If that was the case, why not just be open and bring them both to the table... Since everyone was so satisfied?"

"Come on now, Doc—you know that would've cau-

25

sed way more harm than good."

"My point exactly... You knew your wife wouldn't have openly accepted you being involved with another woman. Yet, you still found a way to justify doing so."

I shrugged my shoulders, really not giving a fuck. "Shit, if you say so... It is what it is."

Dr. Bishop took a long sip from her coffee cup, eyeing me the entire time. "When you choked Trina, was that your first time getting violent with her?"

"I might've slapped her up once or twice, just playing around."

"You say that as if it's normal for a man to put his hands on a woman in any kind of way."

"I wouldn't say that it's normal, but it's not like it's the end of the world either. Sometimes, when women get out of line, you have to put them back in their place."

"But you didn't feel like that growing up when you were witnessing it, now did you?"

"I didn't know any better back then."

Dr. Bishop nodded her head while logging more information. "I'm going to ask you a question. All I want in return is a simple yes or no."

"A'ight, go ahead."

She leaned back in the chair while folding her arms. "Would you be okay with a man doing that to Denisha?"

I struggled to gather an answer that didn't make me sound either stupid or hypocritical. Dr. Bishop saved me the embarrassment as she interrupted my train of thought.

"You don't have to respond, Mr. Nelson. I think we both know the answer..." She sneered before switching angles. "Earlier, when you painted the disturbing picture of choking Trina, you also mentioned that you didn't get your point across... Can you elaborate on that, please?"

●●●

Trina didn't speak to me for a few months after the

choking incident. She wouldn't respond to my texts and when I called, she'd send me straight to voicemail. I tried popping up at her house but couldn't find her there either. I'd never gone that long without hearing from her. Honestly, I was starting to become concerned.

About six months later, Trina called from an unfamiliar number. She explained that she was terrified after I nearly suffocated her. She also stated that although she loved me, she refused to move forward as my side piece. Trina had plans of having a family of her own, which I totally understood. Amongst other things, she stated that she was still clean and had been doing in-home nursing for an elderly lady out in Inglewood. It was good to hear that she was doing well without me. I wasn't ready to let her go just yet though.

Eventually, I convinced Trina to meet with me. We agreed upon Roscoe's Chicken & Waffles on Pico. That was a spot we'd often sneak to and get a quick bite to eat. I lied and told her that Eve and I were getting a divorce. Her eyes lit up as soon as I revealed the fake news. She told me all she ever wanted was to have me to herself, even if it meant waiting her turn. I didn't give a fuck about any of that. I just wanted to fuck and get sucked like old times.

After Roscoe's, we went to Trina's place. We didn't even get all the way in the door before going at it. She stopped me right before I stuck my pipe in. I'll never forget the words she said in her ghetto tone.

"Baby don't nut in me unless you wanna be a daddy again. I ain't fucked nobody since you, so I took the Nuva-Ring out."

I didn't even respond. Before I knew it, I was balls deep. We were only a few minutes in when my knees began to buckle. I could tell Trina hadn't been sexually active by how tight her box was. I felt the explosion coming but I thought I could hold back a little bit longer. When it was time to blast off, I pulled out, busted on her back, grabbed us both wash rags, and left without even saying bye.

A few weeks later, I got a call from Trina with her asking if I could pick her up from work. I agreed and instructed her to send the address. As I followed the GPS, I realized the address looked familiar. The closer I got to the location, the more my mind tried to pinpoint the association of the street number. When I arrived, Trina was already outside. Just my fuckin' luck, the house belonged to Eve's best friend Monique's grandmother, Ms. Ida Mae. This whole time, Trina had been taking care of a woman who practically helped raise my wife.

Immediately, I motioned for her to hurry into the truck. The last thing I needed was for Monique or nosey-ass Ms. Ida Mae, to see Trina climbing into my vehicle. I put the pedal to the metal until we were safely away from the area. Trina was silent the whole way. The anxiety from the close call had me on mute as well. Once we arrived at Trina's apartment, she hopped out without saying anything.

I rolled down the window. "Damn, work was that bad—you can't even say thank you for the ride?"

Trina turned around, gently tossing something through the window before saying, "Thanks—oh, and congratulations."

I sat there thinking, what the fuck does she mean, congratulations?

The object had fallen between the passenger seat and door. I reached down to retrieve it; and, to my mothafuckin' surprise, it was a pregnancy test with two thick-ass lines going across... Déjà vu at its finest.

● ● ●

"Were your feelings the same as when Eve told you she was pregnant?"

"Shit, worse. I almost shitted myself when I read that test."

Dr. Bishop giggled. "Excuse me. That was inappropriate..." The effects of being tickled must've lingered further. "Okay... Okay, I'm back... Forgive me... In those six years, did you ever love Trina?"

"Fuck no, Trina was my side bitch. I cared about her... Like, I'd never want nothin' to happen to her. But love? Hell nah. That's out."

"Well, it was obvious that she was in love with you... And you did mislead her by saying you were planning on leaving Eve... Not to mention the fact that she told you she wasn't on birth control anymore. Do you see how these things could've caused a bit of confusion?"

"Doc, she knew what it was. That's why she got choked out the first time. She and I having a baby together wasn't supposed to happen under any mothafuckin' circumstances whatsoever."

"Then, Mr. Nelson... Why'd you have unprotected sex with her? Especially after she warned you?"

"What the fuck do you mean? I told you that I pulled out. That shit wasn't on me."

"Sir, I'd appreciate if you watched your tone. I'm right here—there's no need to curse or yell at me..." She shuffled in her seat and continued, "You may not like what I'm about to say and that's okay. But it definitely needs to be said." Dr. Bishop slowly placed her pen and pad beside her chair before calmly leaning forward. "You made a choice... And, unfortunately, that choice didn't favor you. Nobody forced you to have unprotected sex with Trina or your wife at the time, for that matter. Those were decisions you made as a competent adult. At some point, you have to accept accountability."

I wasn't trying to hear that shit and Dr. Bishop was starting to piss me off. "Man, fuck all that. What's done is done. It is what it is."

"That way of thinking is going to be a cancer to your growth and maturation as a man if you don't start addressing it. Avoiding and shrugging situations off when they don't go your way, is counterproductive to that."

"Look, fuck what you're talking about. That bitch

was out of pocket for getting pregnant. So was Eve. At the end of the day, I can't change it, but all this blaming me shit ain't gon' cut it."

Dr. Bishop glared at me like a disappointed mother. She collected the pen and pad from the floor before adding to her series of notes. "Again—there's no need to get belligerent… I'm not blaming you. I'm just trying to get you to see things from a different perspective."

I was too ignorant to understand where she was coming from. "Well, it seems like you're making it like it's all my fuckin' fault."

"Those weren't my intentions at all. And if it came across that way, I apologize… I think it'll be wise to switch gears and move forward."

"Yeah, let's kill that shit."

"So, you find out Trina is pregnant. What happened next?"

● ● ●

I was so fuckin' mad that I jumped out of the truck and chased her into the apartment. She was able to lock me out right before I caught up to her. I banged on the door for about five minutes before she threatened to call the police. On the way back to the truck, I yelled out "Bitch, fuck you and that baby. I hope y'all both die and go to hell." I meant every word of it, too. As soon as I hopped in, I blocked and deleted her contact information.

Random private numbers blew my phone up over the next few weeks. I ignored every last one. It was no way I was about to be a part of raising that child. Trina's stupid ass knew that I wasn't trying to have no more babies. Especially after the way shit went down with Eve. She was right there watching me stress through the whole thing. For her to turn around and pull the same exact shit, was selfish as fuck.

Trina popped up at my job soon after. I wanted to slam her head into the wall. She knew better than to just show up like that. I grabbed her arm and forced her outside before she had an opportunity to cause a scene. Trina's eyes had heavy bags underneath. She looked like she'd lost weight as well even though her stomach bulged a little. It didn't seem like she had much fight left in her at all. I pulled her away from the shop just in case she did.

"Why you been ignoring my calls, Deshaun?" she asked.

"Because you know you was out of line for that pregnancy shit. I told you I wasn't having no babies with you."

She pumped her fist at me. "Nigga, I told yo' scandalous ass that I wasn't on birth control no more."

"Bitch, raise yo' hand one more time and I'mma knock yo' mothafuckin' teeth out."

"That's fucked up. You'd really do that to me? Fareal, Deshaun?"

"Man, I ain't tryna hear all that sentimental shit... Wassup? What do you want?"

"What you mean? I want you to help take care of this baby I'm carrying."

"Check this out... I ain't raising no more babies. Tell you what tho'... I'll shoot you a few dollars for an abortion, help you get a new car, and you can push on about yo' way."

"You didn't say that shit to Queen Eve when she got pregnant, now did you?"

"Bitch, keep my wife's name off yo' lips before I knock it off of 'em... You could never compare to her. This was just a fuck thing. Something fun when shit got boring at home... Come on now, sweetheart, you know I was never leaving my family. If so, I would've done it years ago." As sick as it may sound, watching Trina tear up gave me an adrenaline rush. "Look tho' I'mma cash app you this three-hundred right now, and whatever else the abortion cost let me know, and I'll get that over to you too."

"Fuck you, bitch-ass nigga. I hate you," said Trina through a sea of tears.

31

I taunted her by blowing a kiss. "Bye, Trina."

I turned to go back into the shop, but Trina had something else to say. "Nigga, you might not have a family when you get home. Yo' precious wife's friend tried to check me about fuckin' you this morning... And I told her we was too, you hoe-ass nigga."

Monique must've seen her get into my truck the day I picked her up.

I rushed over to Trina, doing my best not to cause a scene myself. "What the fuck did you just say?"

"You heard what I said. Monique wanted to know how long we've been fuckin' and if I knew you was married."

"If I find out you said anything reckless, I'mma fuck yo' ass up."

Trina's eyes were bloodshot red. "You can't hurt me no more than you already have. I hope God punishes yo' triflin' black ass for all the connivin' shit you've put me through. Me and this baby gon' be straight without you."

By this time, a few of my co-workers came out from inside. I didn't know what all they'd heard, so I let Trina parade off without further incident. Somebody must've heard something because I got laid off the next day. That was the last time I heard from her.

● ● ●

"How long ago was that?"

"A little over two years."

Dr. Bishop jerked her neck to the side. "So, that means you've never seen the baby?"

"Nope, don't want to neither."

"You can't be—"

"—Aye, look. I don't want to keep talking about that Trina shit. As a matter of fact, don't even say that bitch name around me no more."

"May I ask why you feel that way all of a sudden?"

"Because just thinking about all the shit the bitch

32

did still pisses me off."

"In regard to her getting pregnant? Or is there more you haven't mentioned yet?"

"What more do I need to say? That hoe strung me out on dope, got pregnant on purpose, and cost me my fuckin' marriage. Shit, that ain't enough?"

"I understand your frustration. I'm sure the situation had a huge impact on your marriage ending... But Mr. Nelson... You don't think it's a little harsh to put everything on her? From the sound of things, you and Eve already had marital issues prior to her coming into your life."

"Like I said... Shit was good with me and Eve after she saw how much I loved our baby girl. Whatever marital issues we had before that, didn't matter anymore."

"Are you sure she was good? Or is it a possibility she was pretending to be good in order to keep peace within the home? Women tend to do that to prevent the children from witnessing trauma." Dr. Bishop cleverly used that opportunity to pry into my upbringing. She cuffed her chin and crossed her legs. "I'm sure your mom would've done the same thing, right?"

Before even realizing, I shouted, "Fuck no."

I'd fallen right into her trap. "That was a very definitive response. Do you mind going into detail?"

"Yeah, I do mind."

Dr. Bishop took a deep breath. "Fair enough. Forgive me for overstepping that boundary, yet again. I'm sure you'll let me know when you're ready to cross that bridge." She briskly turned through the pages of her notes. "So, after Eve's friend confronted Miss... Out of respect for you, I won't say her name... I'm assuming that's when your marriage spiraled out of control..."

"Originally, no—Eventually, yes"

●●●

I was expecting drama as soon as I got home that

day—to my surprise it never occurred. Now, Eve wasn't the most confrontational person. But I knew she'd definitely flip her top if her best friend told her she'd actually seen me in the act of cheating. So, I was surprised once I entered the kitchen and discovered lit candles aligning the counter tops.

Jhene´ Aiko elegantly streamed through the speakers. A dinner of steak, garlic noodles, and steamed broccoli awaited me at the table. Initially, I hesitated thinking, *'Is this bitch tryna poison me, or somethin'?'*

Then, I noticed a handwritten note positioned next to the succulent meal.

Good evening, my King,

As you can see, I made your favorite. Your bath water has been running since I heard the garage door open. Get full, get clean, and come get this pussy!

Love,

The woman that's gonna suck the soul out of you tonight.

P.S. The kids are with my mom, so don't bother to put a towel on.

At that moment, I knew she hadn't gotten the news yet. A part of me felt kind of guilty. The other part of me was happy she finally decided to spice shit up. I was tired of the boring-ass sex we'd been having. It was about time she stepped her shit up. Maybe if she would've channeled that freaky side a long time ago, I wouldn't have had to keep that crazy bitch, Trina, around for so long. Either way, I appreciated the gesture. With Trina being out of the picture, I was finally able to focus solely on my family.

Several months passed and still no word of the tea being spilled. Eve and I were actually the happiest we'd been since she'd gotten pregnant with Denisha. Our communication was better, we went on weekly date nights to keep things fresh, and the sex was fire. I even scaled back on the drugs and alcohol. For the first time in a long time, I felt like we might actually make it. Then, Eve's hating-ass friend fucked everything up. The fucked-up part is, it wasn't even Monique that told her.

So, it's three of them who grew up together—Eve, Monique, and Na'Tosha. The story goes, Monique told Na'Tosha about my affair after confronting Trina but made her promise not to say anything. Na'Tosha, being the 'hood rat she is, took it upon herself to try to fight Trina one night at In & Out Burger. By that time, I'm assuming Trina was showing, and being the dumb broad she is, told Na'Tosha during the altercation, "Bitch, go tell yo' friend I'm pregnant by her good-fo-nothin' ass husband." Na'Tosha went back and told Monique first—Monique fired Trina right after—Na'Tosha eventually told Eve. Shit was just crazy around that time.

Eve was in a fit of rage when she finally got the news. I couldn't get my foot all the way in the door before trophies and vases flew past my head. I pretended as if I didn't know what was going on, but she'd already snapped. This behavior wasn't like her. Actually, I'd never seen her that angry before.

She darted for the kitchen without saying a word and returned with the biggest butcher knife we owned. I could see the disdain in her eyes. Eve had reached her breaking point. All of the fucked-up shit I'd put her through had taken its toll.

She prowled towards me shivering with the eyes of a woman scorned, "I can't believe you got her pregnant. How could you do this to me?"

I tried calming her down, but it wasn't working. The closer she got, the more I actually thought she might really stab me. I didn't give a fuck how mad she was, I wasn't about to let that happen. As soon as she got in striking distance, I punched her right in the mouth. She instantly dropped to the floor, flinging the knife across the living room.

I retrieved the knife. "Bitch, don't you ever push up on me wit' a knife in yo' hand. What the fuck is wrong wit' you?"

Blood streamed from Eve's mouth as she laid across

the carpet dazed, peeking up at me through defeated eyes. "Get the fuck out, Deshaun. Get the fuck out now."

I understood why she was mad and all, but she should've known better than to run up on me like that. She, of all people, knows my temper is short.

I stayed at a hotel for a few days. When I returned, Eve, the kids, and their clothes were gone. On the mirror of the master bathroom was a note written with lipstick that simply read: *"I'm filing for divorce. You can have the house and everything in it."*

● ● ●

Dr. Bishop dipped her head, removed her glasses, and massaged the bridge of her nose. "Mr. Nelson, what were your feelings as you watched your wife—the mother of your children—who you'd been unapologetically cheating on for several years, lay on the floor, mouth full of blood, because she was distraught over the news that you'd gotten your mistress pregnant? Do you honestly think your actions were merited?"

"Shit, I felt bad, but what was I supposed to do? Just let her kill me?"

Dr. Bishop's voice elevated. "Please, cut the bullshit, okay... When you hurt someone's feelings, you don't get to gauge their response. You knew good and well that Eve wasn't going to kill you. Yet, you still decided to add more damage by violently punching her... Seriously, why do you feel it's okay to take action when you're upset, but when these women do the same, you take it upon yourself to turn abusive?"

"At the end of the day, I'm a man before anything. Ain't nobody about to disrespect me—that's out."

"Disrespect? What about the disrespect you've displayed? Do you honestly think it's fair that you're allowed to huff and puff, disrespecting women whenever a situation doesn't go your way?"

"Fuck all that... Life ain't fair."

"You're absolutely right. Life isn't fair—which is exactly why you're going through what you are now. Your narrative has been created by the karma of your actions. Somewhere along the way you've adopted this notion that demonstrating violence against women is normal. That has to be corrected... But the only way it can be corrected, is by getting to the root of the problem. Whatever pain you're internalizing is causing you to inflict it on others. And the thing about pain is, whenever you store it away, it doesn't actually go away. It just stays in place until your mind revisits that storage space again." Dr. Bishop came and kneeled beside me. "There's a saying in the therapeutic community. 'You can't heal how you show up as an adult if you're not ready to heal the trauma of your childhood.' Mr. Nelson, it's imperative that you tell me how you were treated as a child."

The way she made eye contact gave me a sense of security. Her voice was so calm and soothing. It wasn't hard to see that she was passionate about helping people.

"I'm sure you've noticed me documenting notes throughout our first two sessions. Is it okay if I share my analysis with you?"

"Go ahead," I said passively.

"There are characteristics within your personality that have to change in order to stop making the same bad decisions—starting with the way you behave towards women. The level of disrespect you display is alarming, to say the least. The thing that stands out most is that these are women that you claim to have actually cared about," Dr. Bishop's tone strengthened with every word. "These are women that you knew for a fact cared about you. Both laid on a hospital bed and experienced the closest thing to death in order to bring your kids into this world. Both sacrificed their own self-respect and dignity in order to have a tiny piece of whatever you felt like giving at that moment. Both accepted abuse at the hands of a man whose ground they practically worshiped. And all you've done this entire time is blame, blame, blame. That there, sir, is an illness...You're not healthy. Until you're willing to trace the origins of that illness, you'll continue to damage yourself and everyone else you come in contact with—including your own children."

I stood to my feet and clinched my fist. "Don't speak on my fuckin' kids."

Dr. Bishop didn't back down. She postured to her feet and tapped into her inner Chi-town. "No, I'm gon' speak on yo' f'n kids. All three of 'em at that... I'm not the enemy. I'm here to help you... I'm here because too many of our young, black kings are inflicted with pain, hatred, doubt, darkness, and sadness. I'm here because too many of our young, black kings are masking their misery with sex, drugs, and alcohol. I'm here because too many of our young, black kings are being lost to the penal system. I'm here because too many of our young, black kings are being murdered in the streets by the officers who're paid to protect them... But the most important reason why I'm here, is because yo' f'n kids need their daddy healed so they don't have to experience the same trauma growing up as he did."

Although I didn't appreciate Dr. Bishop attacking me, it wasn't hard to see her compassion towards men. Every word she spoke exuded sincere conviction. Little did she know, my respect for her tripled in that moment despite my urge to clap back.

I sat back down and sipped some water, with my blood still boiling from our exchange.

Dr. Bishop collected herself by grabbing a drink of water as well. "Do you need a minute or two?"

"Nah, I'm good."

She took a seat with a smile as if nothing ever happened. "Okay, let's continue, shall we?" Dr. Bishop retrieved her trusty pen and pad before proceeding. "Let's talk about your childhood, Mr. Nelson. Was your father active in your upbringing?"

My hands were now shaking just as fast as my feet. Sweat flooded from the top of my bald head, neck, and armpits. "Can you repeat that one more time?"

She zoned her radar in and carefully observed my body language before calmly approaching. "What you're experiencing right now is called hyperarousal. It's a fight or flight response. Your nervous system is reacting to a sudden release of hormones throughout your body, causing a severe case of anxiety. Do me a favor... Close your eyes and take five slow, controlled, deep breaths." Dr. Bishop gave a tranquil, rhythmic demonstration of what she was asking for. "Imagine creating a star in your mind but be sure to take your time as you construct each line."

I hated the way my body felt while angry. At this point, I was willing to try anything to offset the un-controllable feeling. "So, I'm drawing a regular five-point star in my head?"

"Yes, each inhale and exhale should represent one line of a star. Don't stop until you complete six stars in total."

I tentatively closed my eyes, doing as instructed. Tension released from my brain as I breathed in and out. The mental exercise relaxed my entire body, similar to a light case of hypnosis. I'd almost fallen asleep by the time the last star was completed.

Dr. Bishop calmly disrupted my focus. "How do you feel, Mr. Nelson?"

I felt so tranquil that I could've kicked my shoes off and passed out right there on the couch. I couldn't let her know that though. "I feel a'ight."

My chill demeanor confirmed that the method had served its purpose.

She peeked at the multi-colored sunray clock mounted on the adjacent wall. "Great... I feel more comfortable wrapping up today's session, knowing you're in a calmer space. With that being said, please keep in mind that this is a marathon and not a sprint. There isn't an overnight solution to healing trauma. All we can do is acknowledge the problem and find coping mechanisms, allowing us to deal with it without compromising our mental health any further... Do you have any questions before we conclude?"

I rose to my feet and headed toward the door. "Nah."

"Well, on that note... I'll see you next week."

I exited the office with mixed emotions. On one hand, I felt attacked. Originally, Dr. Bishop appeared to be just another person who didn't understand me. How is this bitch gon' sit up here and get on me when they were the ones who got pregnant without my permission? What about what they did to me? What about how that shit made me feel?

Everything I did towards Eve and Trina were reactions to things they'd already done towards me. So, why was it that I was the one getting the blame? That shit didn't make sense to me.

On the other hand, I'd be lying if I didn't admit Dr. Bishop was sincerely trying to help. Her empathy was evident from day one. A 5'4", middle-aged lady stepped to a 6'5" man like me when I was used to women nearly crumbling at the sight of my anger. The wild part about it was, at no point did I sense any fear from her direction. That alone proved Dr. Bishop's passion for healing was real. I'd come into these early sessions looking for a way to weasel out. Instead, I exited feeling like there may very well be a couple of things in my life that needed to be reevaluated.

THERAPY SESSION #3

I moped into Dr. Bishop's office after earlier that week, being hit with a double whammy of disappointment. First, I was served with an order of protection stating that not only could I not come within five-hundred feet of Eve and Gary—but the kids as well. I thought it was a real scandalous move of Eve, knowing that my babies were the only thing holding me together. Besides, our beef didn't involve them. And if her new man was so tough, why'd she need the police to get involved anyway? I wanted to sit and wait outside of her place and shoot them both on sight. But that wouldn't have been such a wise idea, seeing that I already had an open case looming over my head.

The very next day after being served, I received a letter from the Los Angeles County Child Support Services Department. Apparently, Trina had filed a claim requesting a paternity test. That bitch had a lot of nerve to think I'd do anything for her or that baby. I wanted to stomp a mudhole in her ass after reading the subpoena, but opted against it for the same reason I'd done for Eve and her corny, Russell Wilson wannabe-ass boyfriend.

My energy was depleted from the roller coaster of emotions that'd been plaguing me since the unfortunate sequence of events.

Dr. Bishop must've seen it written all over my face. "Rough day?"

I nodded my head before flopping on the couch. "Rough week is more like it."

"Well, let's talk about it." She reached into the right pocket of her burgundy wine-colored blazer, retrieving the notepad that withheld my personal business from the other sessions. "Tell me what's on your mind."

I took a deep breath. "Eve filed an additional restraining order against me. I can't come within five hundred feet of her or the kids."

"I can only imagine how that made you—"

I interrupted her mid-sentence. "—And Trina filed for child support. They want me to come in and take a DNA test in a couple weeks."

"I'm sure you're deeply angered by both." Dr. Bishop removed the sports jacket and rolled up the sleeves of her off-white blouse. "But let me ask you a question... If you were in their shoes, what would you have done differently?"

Dr. Bishop had a knack for redirecting things back to my actions. This tactic caused me to see things through a different lens. Whether I wanted to do so or not, was a totally different story.

"I'm not in their shoes though, so I really don't know what to tell you."

"Mr. Nelson, let's be honest. If someone came to your place of residence in the wee hours of the night, unannounced, and caused a bunch of ruckus, you'd want to establish a healthy distance from them as well, right?"

I rolled my eyes. "What does that have to do with the kids?"

"If I had to guess, I'd assume she's afraid you may possibly retaliate during one of the scheduled meet-ups."

"That's some bullshit. She's just being spiteful. Her ass knows good and well I wouldn't put my kids in harm's way."

"How are you so sure she knows that after the behavior you've displayed throughout the years?"

I sucked my teeth with a look of fury in my eyes. "Why are you always making everything seem like it's my fuckin' fault? Not one time have you acknowledged the shit that was done to me."

Dr. Bishop relaxed her posture and spoke in a matter-of-fact tone. "Well, with all due respect, I've given you an opportunity on more than one occasion to share the things that have been done to you. Yet, you've declined each time."

"No, you haven't," I said adamantly.

"I certainly have—in regard to your childhood."

I sighed and slammed the back of my head against the upper part of the couch. "Here you go with that shit again... I'm talking about when it comes to Eve and Trina. It's like you just put the whole damn thing on me."

"I'm not trying to fault you at all. But what I am trying to get you to understand is your circumstances may very well be a result of the decisions you make. No one else has the authority to control you unless you allow them to."

"And all I'm saying is, that shit don't just be on me. They both know exactly how to push my fuckin' buttons."

"Even in an event where a person is deliberately pushing your buttons, you have to tell yourself that a person doesn't have the power to control you." Without breaking eye contact, she scooted her chair closer to the couch where I sat. "See, the part I want you to realize is untreated trauma creates a multitude of buttons. And each one is the size of a balloon. It's important to learn how to minimize those buttons until they're so small that the people looking to push them, can't even locate them... Now, I know it's easier said than done, but we have to start somewhere, right?"

I stared into the distance, picking my teeth with the fingernail of my pinky. "Man, whatever... I just need you to stop making it like I'm the problem all the fuckin' time."

Dr. Bishop softened her eyes and leaned forward. "I

don't think you're the problem—it's the problem that's the problem."

"What does that even mean?" I asked, squinting my eyes.

"The alcohol, drugs, anger, pain—Deshaun, those are the problems. You're just a vessel carrying the burden of all four like a two-ton anchor." Dr. Bishop patted me on the shoulder before returning her chair to its original spot. "Don't you think it's time we remove that anchor?"

I knew exactly what she was hinting at, "I really don't understand why you think talking about my childhood is going to fix anything."

"I don't think—I know," said Dr. Bishop, in a confident tone and straight face. She lightened her delivery before conveying the next message. "Before Eve, Trina, drugs, alcohol, and adulthood, there was a young child who somewhere along the way lost his trust, faith, and compassion for women. At some point, his cries and pleas for comfort were ignored. His innocence and love subsequently transformed into rage and intimidation... I'd like to speak to that child—better yet, I'd like him to speak to me."

A frown forged across my face. "That child died a long time ago."

"I strongly disagree... I see him sitting across from me, frustrated because his heartbeats, Deshaun Jr. and Denisha, have been removed from his life. I see him sitting across from me tormented, deflecting the hurt of his past onto others. I see him sitting across from me stressed over the uncertainty of his pending court case. I see him sitting across from me intransigently convincing himself to ignore the responsibility of his third child."

Dr. Bishop's words pierced my soul so deeply that my face couldn't hide the guilt. I avoided eye contact in order to keep her from noticing. "You can see all that, huh?"

Her lips turned into a warm, comforting grin. "I sure can."

She fingered through the familiar green notepad and landed her index finger on a particular page. "During our last session, you mentioned that the reason you didn't get intoxicated around your children was because you'd grown up in a household where adults did that around you. How often were you subjected to that behavior?"

"Daily," I said, twiddling my thumbs.

"And how many years would you say that experience lasted?"

"My entire childhood, all the way until the day I left for college."

Dr. Bishop inked my response. "At what age did you get involved with drugs?"

I paused before reluctantly responding, "I dibbled and dabbled with weed in high school but never anything beyond that. As far as alcohol, I hadn't even had a beer until college. The hard drugs didn't come about until I met Trina."

"What's your drug of choice?"

"Shit, whatever I can get my hands on," I said jokingly. "Nah, but I smoke weed and snort a little coke here and there, but alcohol, Xanax, and lean are my go-to."

"How often do you use them?"

"Every damn day—the lean is expensive so I'm not always able to afford it, but a Xanny bar and a bottle of reposado tequila is a must."

Dr. Bishop seemed to be holding her breath before she said, "Can I ask you a question without you getting upset?"

"Go ahead."

"What is it that you're running from?"

Her question caught me off guard. "What do you mean?"

"Drugs and alcohol are temporary alleviations. They allow us to cope and escape from issues we're not inclined to tackle head-on. What is it that you're trying to get away from so badly?"

"First off, I'm not running from shit. Secondly, I do

45

drugs because I like to, not because I need to. I can stop getting high whenever I want."

She nodded her head with a snicker before writing in her log.

"What's so funny?" I asked.

"Oh, nothing—but if I had a dollar for every time someone said that, I'd be a very rich woman."

"All I'm saying is, I do the drugs—the drugs don't do me."

"Okay, well, let me ask you this then, Mr. I-do-the-drugs-the-drugs-don't-do-me... Who was doing who the night you got into this jam you're in?" She cocked her head sideways.

"Man, Doc. I don't know who the fuck that was." I said, sliding down the couch, tucking my chin into my chest.

"Mm hmm, yeah, I know. See, there are four signs of addiction—obsession, negative consequences, a lack of control and numero uno, denial. All you need to qualify under is one to be considered an addict. So far, I got you down for at least three."

I tugged on my beard staring at the wall, trying my best to muster a rebuttal for her statement.

"The biggest mistake people make is thinking they are stronger than the substance. It may seem that way for a while, but eventually, it'll catch up—sometimes having dire consequences."

I was planning to get high as soon as I left her office, so all her preaching was falling on deaf ears. "If it gets that bad, I'll just quit."

Dr. Bishop licked her finger before turning the page. "I hear you... But just know, I can't recommend you as a candidate for rehab if you're not willing to admit you have a substance abuse issue."

I jolted to my feet. "My bad, you're right. Maybe I do have a problem. As a matter of fact, I do. Go ahead and tell them to sign me up."

"Yeah, I thought so," She said while laughing. "Luckily for you, we have a lot of ground to cover before rehab is even an option."

"We do?"

"Yes. Rehab is like the finishing touches on a nice car. You know, like the rims, stereo system, and shiny paint job. Therapy is the deep down and dirty under the hood work. It makes no sense to add the bells and whistles if the motor isn't running right."

"I feel you on that."

"Let's get back on track. Were there other people in the house getting high and drunk besides your mom?"

"When did I ever say my momma was getting high?"

Dr. Bishop sensed the shift in my energy. "When you mentioned that you'd grown up in a household where drugs were prevalent, I assumed that your mom was one of the people. Please, forgive me for jumping to conclusions."

Truthfully, my momma was actually the ringleader. Be that as it may, I wasn't ready to disclose that information. Rejecting another one of Dr. Bishop's attempts to unravel my relationship with Momma was the only way to keep my secrets disclosed.

"Let's leave the mom thing alone for now... Would you be more comfortable talking about your relationship with your dad?"

I gathered my feet and sat upright, dispassionate would best explain my feeling. "Yeah, I guess we can do that."

"Great... In one word, describe your relationship with him?"

"Nonexistent," I sputtered out.

"Was it always that way?"

"For the past twenty-six years."

Dr. Bishop angled her arm against her lap in the perfect writing position. "So, that means you haven't had a relationship with him since the age of six?"

"I haven't even seen him since then."

"That's a long time for a young man to go without

his father... Is he still alive?"

"Yeah, the last time I checked."

"Well, do you two at least talk on the phone from time to time?"

"Nope. We haven't spoken since I was twelve... He'll occasionally relay messages through Momma on Facebook but that's about it."

Dr. Bishop aimed her eyes at the ceiling. "Let me get this straight, those two still communicate but he and you don't? How did that come about?"

"When I was six, I was told some things that made me not want to talk to or be around him anymore."

"May I ask what kind of things?"

"Just some wild shit that happened between him and Momma during their marriage."

A sly grin appeared on Dr. Bishop's face. "And let me guess, these things were told by your mom?"

I didn't appreciate the way her question came a-cross. "Yeah, but why'd you say it like that?"

"No reason... No reason at all."

Dr. Bishop dived back into her notes while rocking her head side to side. "Did your mom have a tendency to paint him in a negative light?"

I took a few moments to process her question. "Yeah, I guess you can say that, but shit, she was just tel-ling the truth."

"The truth? Or her truth?" asked Dr. Bishop, with her eyebrows raised and a lateral stare.

She continued before I could respond, "How was you and dad's relationship before mom's talk?"

I whistled before taking the trip down memory lane. "To keep it solid, he was actually my hero once upon a time."

"Ah, so Dad was little Deshaun's Superman? Can you give me a description of what he was like?"

"He was tall, strong, funny, and loved sports. We'd go to the Golden State Warriors game every time he came in town. He'd even let me sit on his lap and handle the steering wheel as we drove around the parking lot." A smile surfaced. "The whole time I really thought I was the one making the car go. Those are probably the main things that I remember about him."

"How old were you when they divorced?"

"I was a baby, but he'd come visit from Texas a few times a year—up until I found out what he really was about."

Dr. Bishop rested her index finger against the side of her nose while clutching her chin. "How much of what your mom told you do you remember?"

"All of it," I said without hesitation.

Dr. Bishop dropped the pen and pad in her lap, giving me her undivided attention.

● ● ●

It was spring break 1993, and my dad had been in town from Texas the entire week. Pops, as I use to call him, would pull out all the stops when he was in town. This particular time wasn't any different. We rode go-karts, fished at the lake, hit up Chuck E. Cheese, and swam in his hotel's pool. I even got new outfits and the latest Jordan sneakers. Every night we'd eat at whatever restaurant my appetite called for. I cried like a baby when it was time for him to go back home. I begged him to stay one more day, but he explained that he had to get back to work so our fun times could keep rolling in the future.

When he guided me to the apartment, Momma was standing in the doorway wearing a purple terry cloth robe, oversized rollers, with a cigarette resting between her lips. She'd always have the same stank look on her face whenever Pops was around. Her look intensified as I cried, asking him when I could come live with him. Momma yanked me by the arm, forcing me into the house before I could even say bye.

She took one last drag from the Newport and flicked it past his ear saying, "My son ain't never coming to live with yo' deadbeat ass," and slammed the door.

At the time, I didn't know what a deadbeat was, but she sure did refer to him as that a lot. I stared out the window, wailing as his car slowly disappeared down the block.

Later that night, Momma called me into her bedroom. The tone in her voice led me to believe I was in trouble. So, I was surprised when she signaled for me to lie next to her. She was sipping an Old Milwaukee's Best beer and watching the Lifetime Movie Network. I wrapped in the covers, cuddling as close to her as possible.

Momma rubbed her hand across my head and asked, "You want to hear a story about your dad and me?"

I nodded yes, excited to hear what she had to say.

"Your dad and I met in Fort Bragg, North Carolina on the Army base. Swish is what they used to call him. He was the best basketball player on the entire compound. I knew exactly who he was before we were properly introduced." She smiled from ear to ear. "He was so fine with his stuttering, country ass. I told myself, 'I'mma have me some of him one day.' We'd wave at one another in passing and eventually he built up enough courage to approach me. We exchanged numbers and began dating shortly after.

"I soon moved out of my apartment and into his. Within a year we were married. Things were going good but moving really fast. I started to notice things about him that I hadn't before, like his temper for example. Your daddy was so competitive and would get mad at the smallest things."

Momma's smile turned into a grim frown. "One day, we had a group of friends over for game night. We were playing men versus women charades, and our team had beaten the guys three games in a row. Your daddy sat in the corner pouting as if he'd lost his best friend. I playfully approached him, rubbing the victory in his face a little bit. That's when this happened." Momma pointed to an old scar right above her eyebrow. "He backhanded me so hard that I flew into the kitchen counter. Our friends calmed the situation down, but the damage had already been done. I was so hurt and embarrassed. I couldn't believe he'd done that to me. I packed my bags and was ready to go back to California. He begged—and begged—and begged me to stay. And, for some strange reason, I stayed—and stayed—and stayed as the beatings just kept coming."

I interrupted the story, with a heavy heart. "Pops really used to hit you?"

Momma giggled as if I'd said something funny. "Chile—Did he? Your daddy would beat on me for any reason whatsoever. One time, he grabbed me by the back of my head and banged it into a wall so hard that I couldn't see straight for weeks. He even accused me of having sex with the neighbor, mailman, pizza delivery guy, or any other man that spoke to me. Boy, your daddy is not the man you think he is, that's for damn sure."

Rage surged through my little veins. I couldn't believe Pops would do that to Momma. I felt bamboozled. He clearly wasn't the hero I thought he was.

Momma wasn't done exposing the villain in him. "I'd finally had enough of his shit. I started secretly filing paperwork to transfer to a base in Northern California. I knew if he found out, he might've killed me. I did everything in my power to keep it low key. The transfer got approved two months later. I bought a plane ticket to leave the following week. I didn't care about my clothes, shoes, or anything else. I just wanted to get the fuck away from his ass.

"The night before my flight, I started feeling lightheaded. I tried to walk to the refrigerator to get some water and fainted. I woke up in the hospital with his ass right next to me. Shortly after, the damn nurse came in saying that my bloodwork had come back fine, but we're going to be parents. Come to find out, I'd been carrying you around for three months. I was so mad that I could've fainted again."

"You weren't happy that I was going to be born?" I asked with the eyes of a sad puppy.

Momma kissed me on the forehead. "Baby, I wouldn't trade you for nothing in the world—but I certainly did not want to have a child with that dumb, country, cowardly, fake, pathetic, punk, little dick, stupid-ass mothafucka."

My ears weren't prepared to hear that response.

Momma took a big chug from her beer can. "My plan to creep back to California was going to be a little tougher than I thought. But I was determined to get far away from him. Do you know your nothing-ass daddy had the nerve to say, 'I know you want to go back home. Just give me my son and you can go ahead. We don't need you.' It wasn't no way I was giving you up, but it did further prove that his ass was crazy.

"As soon as you were old enough to get on a plane, I packed us a bag and hopped on the first flight out. I didn't even report to the base that I'd transferred to because I was afraid he'd find us. We went to live with your granny in West Oakland until I was able to get a job and find us a place. I immediately filed for divorce and for full custody. If it wasn't for the state granting him visitations rights, I would've never let him come anywhere near us."

Momma polished off the rest of her brew. "I said all that to say your daddy is a woman beater. I still have the bruises to prove it in case you don't believe me." She pointed to multiple spots throughout her body revealing dark marks against her butter pecan complex-ion. "Tiffany's daddy ain't shit either, but at least the punk bitch keeps those child support checks rolling in. But see, deadbeat-ass Chauncey strolls in town two or three times a year flashing money and gifts like his ass is all high and mighty. The whole time, his good for nothin'-ass is fifteen thousand dollars behind in back child support." Somehow, she shifted her wrath towards me. "So, you can sit around here and cry like a little sissy over his bitch-ass all you want. You ain't never going to Texas. He's lucky I even let him see you—period. I'm yo' momma got-dammit. I'm the one who takes care of you. I put a roof over your head, clothes on yo' back, shoes on yo' feet, and food on the table all year around—not just when I feel like it. That mothafucka' don't run shit but his crusty-ass mouth... Now take yo' lil musty ass in there and get in the shower."

I slumped out of Momma's room perplexed. The person she described seemed nothing like Pops. But I couldn't ignore the aftermath of his beatings riddling her body. The man who I'd idolized was now public enemy number one. From that point forward, I never looked at him the same again.

●●●

"Thanks for sharing that. Connecting the pieces of our past is essential for our growth." Dr. Bishop took a sip of water. "I'd like to ask you a question though—is that okay?"

"Go ahead."

"Do you think it was appropriate for your mom to share that story with you at such a young age?"

"Shit, age shouldn't matter when you're exposing someone, right?"

"In no way am I condoning or excusing your dad's alleged behavior. However, I do think hurt parents have a tendency of giving one-sided versions of the truth, in order to demonize the other parent."

"So, basically, you're saying she lied," I ripped off.

"That's not what I'm saying."

"So, what are you saying, then?"

Dr. Bishop collected herself, "What I'm saying is, a child shouldn't have to bear the burden of their parent's dysfunction—especially regarding events that may or may not have taken place before they were even born. The sad part is, parents rarely realize the long-term psychological effects that speaking down on one another has on a child. Look at you, for example... A man who you once revered, to the point you referred to him as your hero, has been ostracized from your life for twenty-six years due to a story—something that happened before you even knew how to ride a bike."

Her response left me speechless. I stared at my fingernails trying to think of a comeback.

She decreased her voice decibels before continuing with her position. "Think about how torn you are now after not seeing your kids for a couple of weeks. Now, multiply that by twenty—six—years. Even if those egregious things your mom spoke of are one hundred percent true, does that equate to a lifelong ban for someone who absolutely adored you when given the opportunity?"

Dr. Bishop waited for a response, but I didn't have one.

"Mr. Nelson, we're all villains in someone's story. You're experiencing that firsthand with Eve and Trina. But does that mean your rights as a father should be stripped away forever?"

I slowly shook my head side to side, while continuing to fidget with my nails.

"I don't think it's fair for a person's past to indict them with a life sentence. People grow, heal, repent, and eventually, mature. I'm sure there was so much knowledge, wisdom, and life-learning experiences that your dad would be more than proud to share with you. Don't you think you could use some of that right about now?"

"So, I'm supposed to just call him after all these years and pretend like shit's all good?"

"Of course, not... Things like that take time. Nonetheless, I do recommend extending the olive branch. If what happened between him and your mom means that much to you, then ask his side of the story. That way, you can use your own assessment in order to determine what's factual. Otherwise, just focus on you two and the possibility of establishing a bond going forward."

Yeah–yeah–yeah, I thought to myself.

"Is that something you might be interested in doing?"

"I don't know, Doc—I'mma have to think hard on that one."

"Fair enough, no need to make such a big decision so soon. Marinate on it for a minute. I do want to share a quote before we wrap up today's session. 'There's no present like a father's presence.' That statement couldn't be truer, especially within the black community. There's no way to redo the time you've been apart but hopefully the love from before will propel you two to the next level." Dr. Bishop continued, "Speaking of a father's presence... what are you planning to do about Trina's paternity request?"

I skyrocketed from the couch and headed straight for the door, "Whoa, well look at the time, Doc. Gotta go before traffic gets bad. You know how the one-o-one gets around this time. Bye—see ya next week."

Dr. Bishop nodded and cut her eyes. "Mm hmm. Yeah, I know. See you next week, Mr. Nelson."

THERAPY SESSION #4

I glided into the lobby, ready to see my therapy crush. For the second week straight, she was missing in action.

"Doc, what happened to the little cutie with the dreads? I haven't seen her the last couple sessions."

"Well, good morning to you too, Mr. Nelson," she said with a brusque undertone.

"My bad, good morning."

"Nia's off on Tuesdays by the way."

"Since when?" I asked with a scrunch on my face.

"Since she realized you were going to be all in her grill every time you came in. Now sit yo' butt down and let's get started." She nudged me in the back.

I grabbed a bottle of water from the mini fridge, "Tell her she can run, but she can't hide."

"You mean the same way you ran from that question last week?" she asked, while gathering her pen and pad.

I dove on the couch and played dumb. "What question was that again?"

"You know exactly what question I'm talking about. Please, stop."

"You're a little feisty today, Doc. Is everything okay? Do we need to switch roles for the day? You can sit on the couch and I'll sit in the chair and ask you all the personal shit." I cheesed, trying my best to get her to smile.

After several seconds, she finally smiled back. "Boy, hush so we can get started. It's session number four. The gloves are coming off today."

"Is that why you have on jeans and a t-shirt?"

"You'll see why in a little bit. On another note, I'm glad you're in a good mood today. Try to keep that same energy when I ask you the tough questions." She cleared her throat with sarcastically, peeked out the side of her frames, and crossed her legs. "So—about this paternity test."

I slinked down in my seat. "I haven't even thought that far yet. All this shit is coming at me so fast, Doc."

"Well sir, whatever you choose to resist will always persist. This baby situation isn't going to just disappear and the longer you wait, the more complicated it's going to get."

I rubbed my temples trying to release the built-up tension. "Yeah, I hear you."

"That child not only needs, but deserves, to have a father present in its life—let's not allow negative history to repeat itself, okay," said Dr. Bishop before winking. "Did the paternity subpoena have the child's name on it? I hate to refer to a precious baby as it."

"Yeah, his name is Déjaun… Déjaun Anthony Nelson," I mumbled while swiftly tapping my foot against the floor.

She was all smiles like a kid in a candy store. "Aww, that's an adorable name. I'm sure someday you'll both make each other proud."

"Nah, I doubt it."

"Shouldn't we be a little more optimistic?"

"Fuck being optimistic. That bitch, Trina, just wants to ruin my life. I don't care what that test says. I'm not giving her or that child one mothafuckin' penny." Before I knew it, I was on my feet. I paced around the office, fiercely pounding my fist against my palm, while Dr. Bishop sat calmly in her seat paying close attention to my sudden outburst. "Eve got these punk-ass courts in my business, I might be going to prison, can't even see my fuckin' kids. And now this hoe, Trina, after everything I've done for her, comes out of left field asking for child support for a fuckin' baby I didn't even want in the first place," I barked at the top of my lungs. "Fuck both they asses. I swear this shit ain't coo'. I hope they both go to hell with gasoline thongs on." My fists were clinched, teeth gritted, and shoulders tensed so high they touched my ears.

Meanwhile, Dr. Bishop simply sauntered over to a small closet door located in the corner of her office. She fetched a barely used pair of Nike Air Max and swapped out her perfectly crafted leopard print flats.

"Follow me," she said in a definitive tone, before strutting out of her office and in the direction of the elevator.

As we entered the elevator, Dr. Bishop pressed the rooftop button, leaning against the side wall. "The behavior you just displayed is known as Intermittent Explosive Disorder. It involves sudden episodes of impulsive, aggressive, violent behavior and verbal outburst in which a person overreacts to a certain situation. I've noticed you administering this behavior throughout your stories and multiple times in person."

She pushed her hand forward once the elevator door slid open. "After you."

On the other side of a glass door was a huge, empty parking lot, with only a few cars scattered in random stalls.

Dr. Bishop escorted me to a blocked-off area with orange hazard cones surrounding the perimeter. "This is why I have on jeans and a t-shirt."

Aluminum bats, sticks, bricks, glass, and pottery aligned against the cones.

"Anger is a triggered emotion, which means it's unavoidable. With that being said, we have to respect its power by giving it a very small window of our time. Otherwise, it'll consume our entire day."

She reached down and lifted one of the cones. Underneath were a hard hat, safety goggles, and protective gloves. "I recommend allocating a max of twenty-minutes to anger. When something ticks you off, take a few deep breaths, find a secluded area, whip your phone out, and set a timer. In those twenty minutes, kick, punch, yell, cry, or whatever else you do when angry. But once that timer goes off, you must compose yourself and go back to your normal activities. The key is to only give anger a crumb of the overall pie that makes up your day." Dr. Bishop nodded in the direction of the equipment. "What are you waiting for? Your twenty minutes started the moment we stepped off the elevator."

After putting on the personal protection equipment, I grabbed a bat and began swinging. Every swing represented a different aspect of my past that brought pain and anger. Tears streamlined down my face as I bashed objects that I'd mentally replaced with the faces of all the people who'd harmed me throughout the years.

"There you go... Let it all out... Don't be afraid to hear your cries," shouted Dr. Bishop from the sidelines.

I smashed each object, swinging the bat left, right, up, and side to side, as if my life depended on it.

"Talk to it... Make sure it knows why you're so angry," screamed Dr. Bishop over the sounds of broken glass and porcelain.

At that moment, my mind went into a trance as I flung the bat like a mad man. "Eve, fuck you and that restraining order. Bitch, I want to see my kids."

"Let it out," added Dr. Bishop.

"Trina, leave me the fuck alone. I didn't ask for no more fuckin' babies."

"There it is, keep going."

"Pops, where the fuck were you when I needed you? Why didn't you fight harder to be in my life?" I roared.

"Yes, that's it... Keep going... Pour it out... Pour it

60

out, Deshaun... Pour it all out."

I was completely at the mercy of the bat.

"Fuck you, Bobby Ray. I hate yo' mothafuckin' ass. Die, bitch... Die."

"There it is... You're doing great... Get it all out."

"Auntie Tika, why the fuck did you bring him around us? And why'd you make me do that—to that baby?"

Feelings I'd buried for decades resurfaced with every swing. Incredible Hulk-like strength overtook my muscles as the bat crushed everything in sight.

"Momma..." The tears were flowing now. "Why weren't you there to protect me? Why didn't you believe me when I told you? Why didn't you just listen to me? Why'd you make me feel so got-damn worthless?" The last few swings had taken everything out of me. I tossed the bat across the lot and dropped to my knees.

Dr. Bishop rushed over and held my head against her bosom while I sobbed away. She placed my right hand over my heart and repeatedly whispered, "It's okay, hon'... Embrace the feeling... Then, release it from your heart."

I clinched tight to her waist with ever-flowing tears dousing the bottom of her t-shirt. The last minutes of my session were spent right there—in that exact position. An unexpected breakthrough had been made. Dr. Bishop finally managed to peel a layer off the thick onion of my past.

THERAPY SESSION #5

I breezed through the lobby as if I wasn't already fifteen minutes late. Dr. Bishop's wooden door was cracked as I tiptoed inside of the plush office. She was already positioned in her seat with notation materials in hand.

"Ah… Mr. Nelson, you finally decided to show up. Glad to have you back—have a seat," she said while tapping her watch.

I shrugged as I made my way to the couch. "My bad, Doc."

If she only knew what all it took to convince myself to return, she'd be happy that I even showed up.

"How have things been since we last met?"

"It's been coo'," I responded. "What about you?"

"Things have actually been pretty good. No complaints at all. Thanks for asking." Dr. Bishop shuffled into position. "Okay, let's get started… Seems like we got over the hump a little bit last week, huh? How did it feel to release that pinned up anger?"

"I can't even lie. It felt good."

She reached out to give me hi-five. "That's terrific to hear. I'm so proud of the way you dug deep and released all of that emotion. You should be proud of yourself as well. That's not an easy thing to do."

"Being able to break shit with a bat and not get in trouble for it didn't hurt neither," I said jokingly.

"I bet…What people usually think is their problem, typically isn't the issue. Here it is your anger has been deemed by others as egotistic rage, and the whole time, you've been harboring feelings of mistreatment as a child. A classic case of the old saying, hurt people hurt people."

She stretched out and grabbed my hands. "So—now that we've successfully reached a cornerstone in your healing, I think it's the perfect time to address some of the things you mentioned during the unleash exercise… Can you please describe your relationship with mom?"

That left the daunting topic I'd danced around for decades. Deep down, I wanted to avoid the discussion at all costs. But I'd been burying my feelings for far too long. I decided to let it out. It was time to open Pandora's Box.

"Depends on what day we're talking about," I replied.

"Can you elaborate on that?"

"It's weird because some days, she's my favorite person in the whole world. And other days, I resent her for all of the things I experienced growing up."

"Interesting, is she the same person now as she was then?"

"Nah, she's actually gotten a lot better."

"In what ways?"

"First off, she's a hell of a grandmother. The kids love her to death. Sometimes, I think they'd rather be with her than me."

Dr. Bishop smiled. "See, that's granny's magic touch. Don't hate."

"I'm not hating at all. It feels good to see her righting her wrongs through them. I just wish me and Tiffany would've gotten some of that growing up."

"Are you saying she wasn't affectionate towards you during your childhood?"

"Affectionate? Hell, nah," I said while laughing. "I mean, she tries to be a little more now, but even then, it

64

seems forced and awkward."

"So, as you've gotten older, she's tried to do things differently. That's a good sign of growth, wouldn't you say?"

"I guess you could say that. One thing I will say is this, if I need anything from her like a ride, something to eat, my laundry done, or even a place to stay, she's there. No questions asked."

"That's great accountability from your mom. Regardless of the past, I know it feels good to know she can be counted on now."

"It does feel good. Especially during the times I'm watching her interact with the kids. I'm not gon' to lie, the shit makes me lightweight jealous sometimes."

"Don't feel bad. Grandparents get to have somewhat of a do-over once the grandkids are born. Showing them tons of love can also double as a way of saying sorry. So, let me ask you this—how would you say you were loved as a child?"

"Not so good," I responded like a shy choirboy after momentarily hesitating.

"Do you remember how old you were when you first felt that way?"

"Since I was about six years old."

"Was there a particular incident you can reference that caused those feelings?"

"There are a lot of things that transpired over the years. It's kind of hard to pinpoint just one."

Dr. Bishop's writing hand hadn't stopped moving since we'd gotten on the topic. "How about starting with the first time you felt unloved... Where were you and what all was taking place?"

"It was in Oakland—at our apartment in the 69th Village."

"Is it okay if we begin there?"

My initial reaction was to get up and leave. Just the thought of opening up about those days sent my angst into a frenzy. I lowered my head and sucked in as much air as possible. But my body was numb and cold, causing my legs to stiffen. After a few seconds, with a lump in my throat the size of a baseball, I lifted my head. "Yeah, that's coo'. We can start there."

● ● ●

Things were so crazy when we lived in the 69th Village. The streets of East Oakland in the early 90s was bad enough. But the things that took place inside of our home, made being outside not so bad. It seemed like Momma always had other people around. Old school R&B played loudly into the wee hours of the night. A combination of crack and cigarette smoke drifted in thick clouds throughout the entire house. St. Ides malt liquor and Seagram's gin filled everyone's red plastic cups. Dominoes slammed against the kitchen table as interchanging groups partied in our apartment like it was a nightclub.

My introduction to violence occurred during this time. One night, Momma's twin sister, Auntie Tika, got into an altercation with her boyfriend, Bobby Ray. The two had lived with us and occupied what was supposed to be my bedroom. That left my sister Tiffany and me to split her tiny room where we shared bunk beds. On this particular night, Bobby Ray decided to shift his assault from verbal to physical. After accusing Auntie Tika of flirting with one of the partygoers, Bobby Ray waited for the crowd to leave, took a bottle of Crystal Louisiana hot sauce, and cracked it upside her head. I was horrified. The sight of my second mom lying in a pool of blood was too much for my six-year-old brain to process. Tiffany, on the other hand, just stood there emotionless. She was only four years old but proved early to be a lot braver than I was.

"See… Look what you made me do," said Bobby Ray in a deep Tennessee accent. He stood over her glaring.

Auntie Tika squirmed as blood gushed from her forehead. At that moment, I ran as fast as I could to

Momma's bedroom. She was in the bed, loudly snoring next to some guy I'd never seen before. I shook her foot, but she didn't budge. She'd been up partying for three days straight so, once she passed out, it was nearly impossible to wake her up.

The stranger popped his head up instead. "What you want, lil blood? Yo' momma sleep."

Feeling afraid and helpless, I accelerated the situation. "Help... Please... Uncle Bobby Ray killed Auntie Tika."

The guy, who I later learned was a notorious Oakland street legend named Dalvin Booker, jumped up, put on his pants, and grabbed a pistol that was tucked underneath his pillow. He stormed into the kitchen where Bobby Ray was strangling the color out of Auntie Tika's pretty, light-skinned face.

"Mothafucka', what's wrong with you, man?" hollered Dalvin Booker.

Before Bobby Ray could respond, a swift swipe of the gun crashed against his mouth, knocking three teeth out, sending blood and plaque flying.

Tiffany stood there and watched the ordeal with a blank face. Nothing ever really seemed to rattle her. I ran into the bedroom and hid inside of the closet. Fifteen minutes later, I heard the sound of walkie-talkies coming from the living room. By this time, Momma had awakened from her slumber, and was screaming at the officers as if they were the ones to blame. I popped my head out of the bedroom in order to see what was going on. Tiffany was on her way in with all of the details her young mind could gather.

"Uncle Bobby Ray is in handcuffs, and that other man is too."

"Is Auntie Tika okay?" I asked.

"I think so, but they're putting her in the ambulance on that stretcher thing," said Tiffany.

Tiffany and I watched through the screen door as Oakland PD hauled Bobby Ray and Dalvin Booker away.

This was the first time I'd ever experienced something so traumatic. Unfortunately, it would be far from the last.

• • •

"Oh my, that had to be a horrific experience. I'm so sorry that you had to endure that... You were six at the time, right?"

"Yeah."

"So, it was your mom, sister, aunt, aunt's boyfriend, and yourself in the apartment. How long had it been that way?"

"My aunt's boyfriend had only been around for a few months, but my Auntie Tika had always lived with us off and on—at least for as long as I can remember."

"If you don't mind me asking... Was it normal for your mom to have guys in and out of the house frequently? You don't have to answer that if it makes you uncomfortable."

"Shit, guys... women... policemen, too. The only thing that was new that day was the physical violence."

"Interesting." Dr. Bishop made another note. "Do you remember if your aunt was hospitalized for long?"

"She had a few bumps and bruises, but we picked her up from the hospital the next morning."

"What about her boyfriend? Did he stay in jail?"

"Damn, I'mma get to all that... Let me finish breaking the story down while I'm in the mood."

Dr. Bishop gave me a stern look that only a black woman could mimic. "My apologies, Mr. Nelson. Please, proceed."

• • •

Two weeks later, Bobby Ray was out of jail, and right back like nothing ever happened. He and Auntie Tika snuggled on the cigarette burn-riddled love seat that'd seen better days, to say the least. Tiffany and I made our way to the bedroom as Momma prepared drinks for the company she was expecting. We figured leaving the room on our own would be better than waiting around to eventually get kicked out.

Tiffany managed to fall asleep after a couple of hours of tossing and turning. Meanwhile, I stared at the wall, doing my best to drown out the sounds of outdated music, and the vibrations of a room full of drunken people bickering about God knows what. After thirty more minutes, I had to use the bathroom.

Bobby Ray spotted me creeping out of the bedroom. He was standing in the doorway of my old room, away from all the chaos.

Before I could get into the bathroom, he motioned for me and whispered, "Come here."

I was creeped out by his thick country accent. Once there, he rushed me into my old room and closed the door. In his hand was a can of Olde English malt liquor. To this day, I can't stand the sight of that gold can.

"You want some?" asked Bobby Ray.

I knew that it wasn't right for me to drink beer, but all the adults loved it so much. I had to see what all the fuss was about. My first mistake was drinking from the can like it was a glass of Kool-Aid. I was already three gulps in before the bitter aftertaste of the disgusting adult beverage registered inside of my little undeveloped brain.

Bobby Ray giggled as my face contorted. "This time, hold your nose when you drink it and it'll taste like root beer."

I don't know why I believed him. I pinched my nose and guzzled until I couldn't take any more. The fumes from the beer burned my throat and nose after I burped.

Bobby Ray's dirty index finger covered both of his lips. "Shhh, I'll be right back." He slithered into the living room. I guess he had to show his face so my auntie wouldn't become suspicious.

The next five minutes felt like an eternity. My head

was spinning like crazy. The taste of the strong, cheap beer made me nauseous. I tried to leave the room but fell after only one step. I felt like I was dying. I crawled on all fours trying to make my way to Momma. At that moment, I needed my protector to save me from this horrible feeling. I screamed as loud as I could, but the only person that heard me over the loud music was Bobby Ray on his way back to finish what he'd started. He entered the room, and I began to cry. My body felt strange, I couldn't think straight, and the cold look in his dingy eyes let me know that I was in serious danger.

"I thought I told you to be quiet boy," grunted Bobby Ray.

He ransacked through a drawer. At first, I thought that he was looking for a weapon to beat me with. I closed my eyes and screamed at the top of my lungs, "Momma." But my cries didn't stand a chance to be heard over Stephanie Mills' "Jesse" blasting through the speakers.

Once Bobby Ray found what he was looking for, he snatched me by my shirt and propelled me to my feet. He held me up to prevent me from collapsing. To my surprise the only things in his hand were a book and small container Vaseline.

Bobby Ray took my right hand and placed it on top. "You swear on the Bible you not gon' tell?"

At this point I didn't know what was going on. My equilibrium was off, stomach was in knots, and I was willing to say or do anything to get to my momma. So, I agreed. I tried to make it to the door, but he tugged my arm. He told me the only way to feel better was to let all the beer gas out of my butt. Even as a tipsy six-year-old, this advice sounded strange. He advised me to spin around five times and fart. After a couple spins, I collapsed onto the floor. My head was so dizzy that I vaguely noticed his silhouette hovering over me. I felt like a victim in a horror movie about to take his last breath. My final attempt to crawl was unsuccessful.

Bobby Ray slid my Batman, Fruit of the Loom underwear to the side, greased his nasty thumb, and rammed it into me. My whole body locked as the shock from the unfamiliar feeling immobilized me. The excruciating pain was so unbearable, I couldn't breathe. I prayed that Momma or Auntie Tika would bust through the door and save me, but it never happened. It was just me, and this monster that I considered an uncle, isolated from any safety that I could've depended on. The atrocious act that seemed to last an eternity, but realistically was less than a minute or so, had finally come to an end. After gasping for air, the effects of alcohol and torture made me sleepy. Bobby Ray picked me up and carefully carried me into my room.

The last thing that I remembered hearing before passing out was him saying, "Don't forget that you swore on the Bible. If you tell anyone, God's going to strike you, Tiffany, and yo' momma down."

The next few days were extremely uncomfortable for me, figuratively and literally. Going to the bathroom was painful. Drops of blood were mixed in with my poop. I wanted to tell Momma so bad but feared that we'd all be struck down if I did. I felt so lost and ashamed. I prayed for God to take me back to that night so I could just go to sleep like Tiffany had. How could I be so stupid? Why didn't I just go to the bathroom like I was supposed to? I hated myself for allowing it to happen. If I wouldn't have agreed to drink the beer, then none of this would've ever happened, right?

I did my best to stay away from Bobby Ray going forward, but there was only so much distance inside of our subsidized housing apartment. Every time Momma or Auntie Tika turned away, he'd stare at me with that awful glower and whisper, "shhh." I tried to just forget about it. I figured that maybe if I pretended like nothing happened, somehow the slate of shame and guilt would be wiped away.

● ● ●

Dr. Bishop's pen blazed against the paper as she made sure not to leave anything out. The empathy in her eyes made me feel less ashamed than I'd expected. I wiped tears from my face with the back of my hand.

She hurried over to console me. "My heart bleeds for you, sweetie. You didn't deserve what happened to you. Was that Bobby Ray's first time molesting you?"

I lowered my head. "Yeah."

"Did the abuse happen often?"

"Nah, it only happened once."

"I couldn't help but notice the unfair blame you placed on yourself for what occurred. Do you still feel that way?"

I carefully pondered her question. "A little bit... But I mostly blame Momma and Auntie Tika."

Dr. Bishop leaned forward and tapped her chin with her finger. "Can you tell me exactly why you blame them— and then yourself?"

My nostrils flared. "What the fuck do you mean, why? It was Momma's job to protect me from shit like that... Why didn't she see that shit coming? And Auntie Tika should've never had that bitch-ass, weirdo nigga around us in the first place," the bass in my voice roared and rumbled throughout the room.

Dr. Bishop just sat there relaxed and patiently waited for me to finish my tirade. "My apologies if stirring up your emotions offended you, but I actually triggered that response for a reason. You see, there wasn't a single mention of why you blamed yourself in that entire outburst. You gave very specific reasons of why you felt they were at fault, but didn't do the same for yourself... Do you know why, Deshaun?"

At this point she had me confused. "No, why?"

"It's because you're not at fault. That's just the way trauma works. It tricks your mind into feeling guilty about being victimized and sadly forces you to carry the burden as if you'd asked to be violated. There wasn't anything that you could've done to prevent Bobby Ray's actions. Whatever pedophilic urges he was having would-'ve brewed over at some point. The guilt that you're feeling doesn't belong to you, and I'm going to do my absolute best to help you remove it from your mind."

Everything she said sounded on point. However, it didn't change the way that I viewed the situation. I still felt like it never would've happened had I just ignored him and went and used the bathroom.

"Did you ever tell anyone about what happened?"

"Yeah... But I really wish I wouldn't have."

"Do you mind explaining?"

I stretched my arms far apart as I sprung from the couch, "Not today, Doc. It's almost that time anyway."

We still had twelve minutes left. But that was all I could handle for the day.

"Thank you for being so open. I really appreciate the way you've grown each session. You should be very proud of yourself..." She pressed her lips together and motioned towards the door. "See you next week."

THERAPY SESSION #6

I bounced into the lobby with extra pep in my step.
The white-bitch Donna had finally gotten her settlement
check from a car accident she'd been involved in months
prior. What was hers was all mine, so I knew I had a few
thousand waiting on me as soon as the money cleared. I
even planned on being nice by leaving her a few dollars
instead of taking all of it like I'd normally done.

I trekked past the front counter, en route to Dr. Bishop's office.

"Have a seat, sir. Dr. Bishop will be out in just a
second," said the white, heavy-set, cross-eyed receptionist who'd been there since dreadlock baby switched
off days.

I stared her in the good eye, nodded, and took a
seat. Usually, I'd just skip past the desk and prance straight into Dr. Bishop's office. But I really wasn't in the
mood for confrontation. My week had been going pretty
well and I wanted to keep it that way.

The last session had definitely taken its toll on me.
Dr. Bishop's persistent prying took me back to a time that
I never wanted to remember. Sadly, I knew it was only the
beginning.

Minutes later, Dr. Bishop appeared from her office,
leading one of her patients to the exit. Her sweet, invig-

orating aroma filled the entire lobby, "Good morning, Mr. Nelson. I'll be right with you."

I took that as my cue to go inside her office and get comfortable. On the way in, I shot Big Bertha the bird for the way she got at me earlier. She's lucky I didn't curse her ass out.

I grabbed an apple, water, and two granola bars from the snack area before kicking my Timberland boots off and lying on the couch.

"Making yourself at home as usual, I see," said Dr. Bishop as she creeped in, closing the door behind her.

"You already know," I blurted out with a mouth full of granola."

"How was your week?"

"My week was good."

"Good, huh? Not just coo' or a'ight? We truly are making ground, aren't we?" she said while taking her seat.

"I see you got jokes this morning."

"Just a little."

I swigged down some water. "Why do I have a feeling it's about to get serious real fast tho'?"

Dr. Bishop clicked the cam of her pen and sifted through the notepad. "Because you already know the drill, that's why." Her playfulness was clearly turned up that morning. "So, let me see—where did we leave off— oh, here we go, right here. Last week, we left off with me asking if you'd told anybody about what Bobby Ray did to you. You said, 'yes but you wish you hadn't'. Is it okay if we pick it up there?"

I dusted granola crumbs from my beard and chest. "Damn you don't waste any time, do you? Yeah, I guess we can start there."

●●●

A couple of months later, we had an assembly at school. Every grade met in the auditorium, as a guest made an important announcement. The speaker was an officer from Oakland police department's special victims' unit. The policeman spoke about the many different tactics' child predators use in order to sexually abuse children. He also stated that these abusers typically used strategies to make the victims feel like they were at fault and even made claims of them potentially getting in trouble if they ever told anyone. This sounded all too familiar. Just when I was starting to put it behind me and enjoy the beginning of my second-grade school year, this officer came in and refreshed my memory.

He closed his speech by saying, "If there's anyone in the audience who's been a victim, please don't feel bad. You're not alone. We're here to help put the bad guys who've done this to you in jail. And most importantly, we're here to keep you and your families safe. In order to accomplish this, we need you to be brave and privately tell a teacher that you trust."

In an auditorium filled with at least a few hundred students, I felt like he was personally talking to me. The only problem was, the word brave and I didn't mix. That was more of Tiffany's forte. I was as timid as they came. My own shadow pumped fear into my cowardly little heart. But somewhere deep inside, I had to find the courage to do the right thing. Bobby Ray deserved to be in jail with all the other booty bandits of the world. And at that moment, I told myself that I was going to be the one to do it.

Shortly after the assembly, I approached my favorite teacher, Ms. Lee. She was a beautiful, African American lady in her early thirties. Her long, silky, dark-brown hair was always curled in perfect spirals without a single strand out of place and her perfume smelled like a combination of vanilla and brown sugar. I often dreamed of us getting married someday. I even started saving my loose change to buy her a nice ring. Beyond all of my puppy-love fantasies, I knew that Ms. Lee was someone who I could trust.

Once I shared the details of the horrific incident

with her, she began to cry. She pulled me in closely and cradled me like a newborn baby. I was in such a blissful state of mind that I really didn't care about the Bobby Ray incident anymore. Ms. Lee ensured me I was safe, and everything would be okay. She remembered I had a younger sister and asked if she'd been assaulted too. I told her I wasn't sure. The next question she asked was if my mother was aware of it. My response was no. After squeezing me one last time, she made a phone call and escorted me to the principal's office. The officer from the assembly was already there when we arrived. Ms. Lee instructed me to tell him the same exact story that I'd told her moments prior. A few minutes later, Tiffany was brought into the office by her kindergarten teacher. She sat beside me oblivious to what was taking place.

I felt like a hero. Thanks to me, Bobby Ray was finally going to get what he deserved. I knew that Momma would be proud of my courageous act, and Auntie Tika didn't have to worry about being beaten up anymore. Being brave didn't seem so hard. The officer assured me that from now on, Tiffany and I would be protected.

As we sat in the office, waiting for Momma to pick us up, another officer came in. She introduced herself and asked Tiffany to come with her. Tiffany and I locked eyes as the female policeman took her away. Something wasn't right. Immediately, I began to worry. I jumped up and followed them.

The male officer firmly gripped the sleeve of my school-issued sweater. "Everything is fine. You're coming with me and Tiffany is going with Officer Tate. Don't worry, we're taking you both somewhere safe."

That wasn't a part of the plan. I thought that Momma was coming to get us, and Bobby Ray was going to jail. Instead, my sister and I were being separated from each other and taken away from our home. To make matters worse, it was all my fault. My heart started beating fast as my eyes filled with tears. I felt crossed by not only the officer, but Ms. Lee as well. This was where my distrust in authority figures originally stemmed from.

As the police cruiser drove me away, my dejected voice whimpered, "Please officer, can you call my momma."

The officer ignored me and turned up the music. He wasn't as nice as he'd been in the Principal's office.

Twenty minutes later, we arrived at an old yellow house in an unfamiliar neighborhood. The trees were perfectly trimmed, and the yards were neatly manicured. It was a huge difference from the concrete jungle of the 69th Village.

The officer saw me into the doorway and drove off. An older black lady greeted me, introducing herself, but I didn't care to remember her name. The house smelled like mothballs and Bengay. Plastic covered furniture and antique trinkets decorated the large living room space. The lady asked if I was hungry. I shook my head no, wiping snot away.

"Well, there's liver and onions in there if you change your mind." She handed me a blanket and lead me into a small room located upstairs.

"Is my momma coming to get me soon?" I asked, trying my best not to breakdown.

"Baby, your mother isn't coming. This is your new home until they find you permanent placement."

I collapsed to my knees and prayed, "Lord, please show Momma how to get here."

The lady sighed on the way out of the cold, pungent, pocket-sized room.

I didn't get much sleep that night. I stood by the window, hoping that Momma's dark green Nissan Datsun would come sputtering up to save me. Each car that passed by was a reminder of the huge mistake that I'd made. I felt so bad for Tiffany. She hadn't done anything to deserve being taken away. I was the one who drank the beer. The punishment should've only happened to me. I prayed that she was safe wherever she'd been taken to.

The sounds of crickets chirping gave me an idea of

the time. My eyes were burning but my mind was too cloudy to fall asleep. Usually, Saturday mornings meant riding bikes with my friends. But on this day, I questioned whether I'd ever see them or my bike again.

The old lady came into the doorway shortly after. "Good morning, there are cornflakes in the kitchen if you're hungry."

"Thanks, but I'm okay," I replied while rubbing my sleep deprived, dreary eyes.

"Baby, the first night is always the toughest. Soon you'll get used to being here. Just give it a little time." She winked before shutting the door.

Get used to being here? I thought to myself.

Just the sound of that statement sent me into a panic. The last bit of energy zapped from my scrawny body. I lay back on the bed and closed my eyes. If I ever needed a blessing, that sure was the time.

After dozing off for a couple of hours, I was awakened by the old lady's voice.

"Deshaun, you have a call."

I dashed to the phone. On the other end was the voice that I'd been praying so hard to hear.

"Baby, are you okay?" asked Momma.

A fountain of tears flooded my face. "No Momma, I'm scared. I wanna go home. Please, come get me."

"They're not going to let me come get you until you tell them the truth."

But I'd already told the truth. Maybe Momma hadn't heard the full story.

"Now, I know you didn't like giving your room to Bobby Ray and Auntie Tika, but making up stories to get rid of them isn't the right way to do things. It's a sin to lie, Deshaun. And if you want God to forgive you, baby, you have to tell the police that you made it all up. That's the only way Mommy can make it all better—okay?"

I didn't fully understand what she meant. In one way, it sounded like Momma didn't believe what I told the officer. In another way, it sounded like my only chance of going back home was to change my story. Either way, I was ready to do whatever it took to get things back to normal. With that being said, I took a deep breath, and tried my best not to cry.

"Okay, Momma. I'm sorry for lying... Can you please come get me now?"

"It's okay, Momma's big boy. No one is mad at you. You can apologize to Bobby Ray when you get home... I'm going to call the officer and get this misunderstanding cleared up. Soon, everything will be fixed like it never happened. Just remember what you have to do... I love you, Momma's little handsome. Bye."

I didn't get a chance to say anything back. I probably wouldn't have been able to even if I wanted. I struggled processing the fact that Momma either didn't believe that it happened, or even worse, didn't want to believe that it happened. There I was, petrified in a foreign environment, being accused of lying by the person whose responsibility it was to keep me out of harm's way. This was the first time in my life that I felt like dying. And somehow, that would become a reoccurring theme.

Whatever Momma said to the detective must've worked. The next day, the two rode together to come get me. I was so happy to see her despite the way I felt about her accusation. The look on her face said that she wasn't too happy about being in this situation, but she gave me a big hug anyway. With Momma's permission, the officer took me into the kitchen to record a statement. She gave me a look that basically said, "Deshaun, don't fuck this up." I smiled to assure her that I wouldn't.

"Okay, Deshaun, tell me exactly what took place that night," said the detective.

I locked my eyes on the table. "Nothing sir, I made the whole story up."

The officer looked at me with a blank face. "Son, the other day, you were pretty graphic about the event that took place... Now you're telling me that it was all a lie?"

"Yes, I made it all up. I wasn't getting any attention

at home so I made up a story hoping that Momma would pay more attention to me." The lie came out so smoothly you would've thought I was a natural.

The officer scratched his head. "Do you realize how much trouble you've caused by doing this? You could've gotten an innocent man sent to prison for a very long time."

I felt so bad for lying. Bobby Ray was a scumbag that deserved to rot in a cage for the rest of his life. But, if retracting my statement meant getting Tiffany and me back home, that's just what had to be done. I thought to myself, Maybe Momma might even tell me that she's proud of me. I rarely heard her say that, so I had the incentive waiting on the other end of the lie. That alone gave me the confidence to finish the interview strong.

I raised my head and stared into his eyes. "I know, Officer. I'm sorry. Can you please forgive me?"

The detective shut off the recording and went into the living room. After briefly talking to Momma, the two returned into the kitchen.

I was so excited to hear Momma say, "Grab your backpack. Detective Bishop is taking us home."

We pretty much rode home in silence. My final relief came when I overheard Momma thanking the detective for allowing my grandmother to pick Tiffany up from the foster home she'd been at. Everything seemed to be on its way back to how it was. Still, that meant Bobby Ray was a free man.

I could feel the tension as soon as we made it home. Momma instructed me to take a bath and get ready for bed. I could tell that she was upset because it was only 6 o'clock and the sun was still out. Bobby Ray's car wasn't there so that bought me some time before having to apologize to the man that'd victimized me. I spoke to Auntie Tika on the way to my room, but she didn't say anything back. Tiffany and my grandmother hadn't made it home yet. That left me in the house alone with two angry twin sisters.

On my way to the bathroom, I overheard Momma and Auntie Tika talking.

Momma asked, "Have you heard from Bobby Ray yet?"

Auntie Tika's voice was low and lacked energy. "Yeah, about an hour ago he called me from a payphone in New Mexico. He should make it to Nashville by tomorrow night."

"I'm so sorry... I can't believe Deshaun would make some shit like that up. If it wasn't for child services being all in my damn business, I'd beat his mothafuckin' ass and let you have whatever was left of 'em."

"It's all right. Once he gets settled, he'll send for me and we'll be back together. Maybe this was God's way of telling us it's time to leave Oakland. I just wish Deshaun wouldn't have caused all this drama."

I turned on the water to drown out what was being said. To have Momma and Auntie Tika totally shut down the notion that I'd been molested hurt more than the actual offense itself. I soaked in the steamy hot bathwater until my skin pruned. I guess I was hoping that the heat would burn away the filth of being violated. My butt wasn't sore anymore, but my heart was. At least I'd never have to see Bobby Ray's black, ugly, Jheri curl wearing-ass face again.

● ● ●

My chest pulsated and I clinched my jaws, balling my sweaty hands into fists. My legs quivered while my feet performed its patented tap against the floor. "Yo, I can't do this shit no more. I'm out."

As I leapt to my feet, Dr. Bishop made an attempt to stop me. "Deshaun, I can only imagine how devastating those unfortunate events were for you. Especially with you being so young when all of it took place. No child should ever have to endure sexual abuse, and the offense is magnified when the disgraceful act is compounded by the dismissal of a parent." Dr. Bishop placed her writing tablet onto the floor, pen behind her ear, and stood with me. "Do me a favor... Close your eyes and take five slow, controlled deep breaths."

I smacked my lips and ice-grilled Dr. Bishop, fighting back tears. "Man, I'm not doing that corny-ass shit."

Dr. Bishop didn't back down from my aggression. Yet, she went about it in a subtle, warming way. She slowly approached me with her hands facing forward, head slightly tilted, and spread her pearly white smile just enough to allow the deep dimples to appear on her pretty face. "Deshaun, please just give it a try."

It was something about the way she went about it that made me feel obligated to listen.

Dr. Bishop gave me a tight, motherly hug before guiding me back to my seat. "In order to repair your feelings, we're going to have to dig them up from the dark place that you've buried them. Bringing them to the light is the only way to properly release the anger. The act of bravery that you've displayed thus far is beyond admirable. Please, give me a chance to help you heal."

I sat back down on the sofa after blowing out a few gusts of frustration.

"Now, on the count of three, breathe with me. One... Two... Three."

I closed my eyes and inhaled. The slow, calculated suctions of air gradually helped center me.

"See, wasn't that relaxing?"

"A little bit."

Dr. Bishop picked up the notepad from the floor. "You ever try talking to your mom about your feelings when you were a kid?"

"She wasn't that type of mother."

"What do you mean by that?"

"We weren't allowed to question nor have an opinion about anything growing up. In her words, 'That ain't a child's place.' So, sitting us down and asking about our feelings didn't happen."

"Can you give me three words to describe how you felt being a child without a voice?"

I took a few moments to regain my composure before slowly uttering a response. "Angry... Hurt... Unimportant."

"I really appreciate you sharing that, Deshaun. I'm sorry to hear that you felt that way growing up. All three of the feelings you just shared are inefficacious to a child's sense of security and belonging." She lightly tapped the ballpoint pen against her chin. "But the feeling that stood out most was the last word, unimportant... Have you ever tried talking to your mother as an adult?"

"A couple of times in my early twenties... But she just shut it down each time. One time she walked off in the middle of me talking and said that I was making her head hurt. Another time, she told me to stop lying on her before I could even address the issue. After a while, I just stopped bringing it up."

"That sounds like a defensive mechanism she's using to avoid reliving that chapter of her own life. I'm sure she's ashamed and has her own untreated trauma festering within. By no means am I justifying any heartache she's put you through. But what I will say is we often forget that our parents are human too. And there's no blueprint or manual on how to be a good parent—or person, for that matter." Dr. Bishop interlocked her fingers. "You think you can convince her to come join us for a session?"

"What? Ain't no way in hell."

"Well, isn't it at least worth a try?"

"I mean—if you say it is—I guess."

Dr. Bishop closed the note tab and slid the pen behind her ear. "Just think about it, okay."

"Sure, I'll think about it."

She checked the time on her fancy watch. "That's all for today. Have a good week, Deshaun."

THERAPY SESSION #7

"Hello."

"What's up Shauny Wauny?" screamed Tiffany through the speakerphone.

"What do you want?"

"Dang. Is that how you talk to your favorite sister?"

"Dude, stop playing. You're my only sister."

"Oops, I knew that," she said cracking up at her own corny joke.

"For someone so smart and accomplished, you sure are goofy as hell."

"Well, thanks. That was so kind of you."

I couldn't help but laugh. "Seriously, what's up? Everything good?"

"Yeah, everything's good—on my lunch break—just checking on you."

"I'm straight—just walked into my shrink appointment."

"Oh yeah. That is on Tuesdays, huh? Well, I won't hold you. I was just calling to say hey."

"Well, hey back at you. I gotta go. Love you."

"Love you, too, bro. Bye."

"Not to be all in your conversation but— who's the lucky lady getting all the love?" asked Dr. Bishop with her hands on her hips.

"Lucky lady—I wish. That was just my sister."

"Tiffany's her name, right?"

"Yep, that's her."

"Are you two pretty close?"

"Absolutely. That's my rock. We've been through hell and back together."

Dr. Bishop took a sip from her latte and smiled. "Your eyes lit up with so much joy when you said that... Tell me a little bit about you guys' relationship."

"Well, first off, she's a moron. Let's get that straight out the gate."

Dr. Bishop chuckled.

"Nah, I'm just kidding. That's my dawg. Whether right or wrong she's always there for me. It's been that way since we were kids."

"It's always good to have someone you can rely on during hard times. If you don't mind me asking, how's her relationship with your mom?"

"It's okay, I guess. We both have similar feelings about the way things were back then, but Tiffany has always done a better job than me at letting stuff go. That's one of the many things I admire about her."

Dr. Bishop straightened in her chair, taking a few seconds to formulate her next request. "Tell me about a period when things were good during your childhood."

I closed my eyes, concentrating hard on pulling up a good memory. "Shit, it was short-lived but if I had to pick a time, I'd say it was when Auntie Tika moved to Nashville. Tiffany and I had our space back. We were really happy about that."

Dr. Bishop wrote away, "As far as mom—did things get better for her as well when your aunt left?"

●●●

Momma was doing way better after Auntie Tika joined her pedophile boyfriend in Nashville. The partying stopped and the strangers disappeared. She even found a good paying job driving buses for the elderly. Tiffany and I were happy to have our own rooms again. It also felt good to see Momma thriving in her new career.

In the early part of the following year, we moved to a block called Caswell. It was located in a small neighborhood known as Brookfield. This community was made of predominately black homeowners, but we lived on a dead-end street with apartments aligned on both sides.

Everyone hung outside and seemed to get along. Kids of all ages played tag, double Dutch, kickball, baseball, and football throughout the day. The adults still drank, played cards and dominoes, but it felt completely different from the 69th Village. It was safer. The people were happier. Parents went to work, came home, and actually did activities with their children.

It was amazing to watch Momma follow suit. She started taking us to the park and played board games with us. We were able to invite company over and have slumber parties. Our clothes and shoes were name brand instead of the Durant Square flea market knockoffs we were accustomed to. Tiffany and I even got a Super Nintendo and new bikes once Momma got her taxes back.

The only bad thing was that we still went to the same school as before. Momma didn't want to take us out because it was too far into the school year. We begged her every day to reconsider. All of our new friends went to Brookfield Elementary. Meanwhile, we were stuck attending a school that required us to wear uniforms. What was the point of having fresh new outfits if you couldn't show them off at school?

My new wardrobe even caught the attention of a cute little girl from up the street. Her name was Kiara. Her brother, Kardell, and I played together almost every day. But she was the one who I wanted to get closer to. I noticed that every time we'd play tag, she'd specifically come seek me out. Whenever I was it, I'd return the favor by chasing her down and tagging her on the butt. Eventually, we sealed our young affections with a kiss behind the building. In those days, that officially made us boyfriend and girlfriend.

One of the teenagers on the block introduced us to a new form of tag called "hide and go get it." This was the X-rated version of the game. All the boys would chase the girls and dry hump them once they were captured. When it was the girls' turn, they'd chase the boys and grab our little wee-wees through the jeans once they caught us.

Every night we'd wait for it to get dark so we could play. On this particular night, things didn't go quite the way I'd planned. My girlfriend, of a week and a half, was chasing after another boy. The homewrecker's name was Josiah. He stayed across the street from me but rarely stayed out after the streetlights came on. Now, we've already established that I wasn't the toughest kid, but I was ready to go to war over my girl.

After watching them chase each other, pulling and grabbing on the other's body parts, I decided to intervene. I stepped to Josiah with my chest out and chin up, like I'd seen in the movies. "Why you grabbing on my girl butt like that?"

Josiah didn't show any fear. He got so close to my face our foreheads were touching. "That ain't yo' girl, bitch-ass nigga."

I was surprised to hear him speak like that. I mean, we were only seven-year-olds. I thought to myself, where'd he learn that from? It was too late to be asking questions. We were face to face and I couldn't back down now. I was the new kid on the block and had to prove that I wasn't a punk. By this time, everyone participating in the game had formed a circle around us. Before I knew it, Josiah pushed me with both hands. The force knocked me to the ground. My immediate reaction was to get up and fight back. I gathered myself and stood to my feet. The kids laughed as I stood in an awkward fighting stance. I honestly didn't have a clue on what I was doing. I'd never been in a fight before and was doing a horrible job of hiding it.

Josiah held his fists up like a skilled professional. It was apparent this wasn't his first rodeo. He lifted his foot slowly, as if he was going to kick me. Once I dropped my hands to block the kick, he clocked me right in the nose with his fist. I instantly dropped to one knee and held my face in agony. Josiah proceeded to bombard me with a barrage of punches to the back of my head. I balled up in a shell, hoping that he'd get tired before one of his punches knocked me out.

Out of nowhere, his onslaught stopped. Through my own cries, I vaguely heard a blunt thumping sound. Josiah let out a painful shriek as he ran home holding the back of his head. I warily uncovered my own head and saw Tiffany standing there with my metal, Louisville Slugger, T-ball bat. Evidently, she'd seen the commotion from her bedroom window and decided to come help her soft, scary, scrawny, big brother from further damage. I probably should've been grateful for her heroics, but I was more embarrassed by the fact that my baby sister had to come to my rescue. Not only did I lose my girl, I lost my respect in the neighborhood before I ever gained any.

Over the next few months, I was constantly reminded that my rank on the totem pole was pretty low. All the kids were athletic, tough, and carried a sense of bravado that I didn't have. I was known as "church boy" because of my passive ways and calm demeanor. Originally, I hated the nickname but after a while, it kind of grew on me. Plus, what was I going to do? Beat up everyone who called me that? Yeah right. After my poor performance against Josiah, even the girls my age felt that they were harder than me.

What I lacked in physical prowess, I made up for in knowledge. Retaining information was something that came easy to me. I might not have been able to play sports very well, but I could tell you everything about them. I studied ESPN everyday like it was a finals exam. I could quote different players' stats like it was the alphabet.

Momma would buy me trading cards when we'd go to the grocery store. Over time, I accumulated an impressive collection. The same kids who ridiculed me, started lining up outside of my door to see what new cards I had. This gave me a greater sense of belonging amongst my peers. They even started convincing their parents to buy them cards as well. A few of the kids built good card books over time, but not like mine. Church boy was the king of the block when it came to that.

It was the start of a new school year and we were all excited. Tiffany and I were finally students at Brookfield Elementary. All the kids on Caswell filed to school as a unit. We'd cut through a hole in the gate leading into an empty field behind my building and make the ten-minute trek. It felt good to be a part of something so unified. Although we had our differences, it was mandatory that we had each other's back once we left the block.

After school, we'd all go to a local recreation center called Ira Jinkins. There, we'd do homework and other academic related activities, as well as play sports, computer games, and shoot pool. This was also a place to socialize with kids from other blocks in the 'hood. Sure, some would scuffle from time to time, but for the most part, everyone got along.

Our family was doing better than ever. I had plenty friends, nice clothes, video games, the best card collection in the area, and was an honor roll student. Tiffany had what seemed like a thousand baby dolls, more clothes and shoes than you could imagine, straight As, and the reputation of not being afraid to swing a bat. Momma was also living her best life. She was getting closer to God, thriving in her career, taking great care of her children, and being more discreet about her extracurricular activities. For two and a half years I experienced the most innocent, happiest, and stable time of my entire childhood.

A week after my ninth birthday, Auntie Tika came to visit from Nashville. Along with her, was my new eight-month-old cousin, Bobby Ray Jr. He was such an active little boy. All my friends raved about his long braids. He had my auntie's pretty, light brown complexion, but in some ways favored his daddy. I could tell that Momma was happy to be reunited with her sister. The identical twins had been nearly inseparable their whole lives. So, it was no surprise to see them jump right back to where they'd left off.

One thing that I was surprised to see was how much weight Auntie Tika had lost. Normally, she and Momma looked exactly the same. Both were about 5'3", 135 lbs. of pure sassiness. Their beautiful butter pecan complexions, and fine hourglass figures, commanded attention from men of all ages. The teenage boys even gawked with lust when the twins strutted by.

For some reason, Auntie Tika looked a lot different. Her frame was so thin that her bone structure showed through her clothes. Her hair was shorter and looked unhealthy. I also noticed a lot of bruises along her arms and legs that hadn't quite healed. The look in her eyes suggested that she'd been through a lot in the past couple of years.

Tiffany and I played with Bobby Ray Jr. as Auntie Tika told Momma stories of how beautiful and peaceful Nashville was. She spoke highly of the great hospitality, the fact that the crime rate was so low, and how the cost of living was only a fraction of what it was in Oakland. It sounded to me like the used car salesman who'd sold Momma that beat up Datsun a couple of years back. Momma just sat there and listened like a child being told a fairytale of a far glorious land. Simultaneously, Tiffany and I eavesdropped praying that she wasn't buying whatever dream Auntie Tika was selling.

After a couple of weeks, Auntie Tika and Bobby Ray Jr. headed back home. We waved as the plane took off on the runway. Honestly, I was happy when they left. Although I loved Auntie Tika, I couldn't forgive her for what Bobby Ray had done to me. And by the way she'd cut her eyes at me, I could tell she hadn't forgiven me either.

"Well, until next time," I said under my breath as the air-craft drifted into the clouds.

The school year had come and gone. Tiffany and I were excited about the summertime events in the neighborhood. We were mostly enthusiastic about our upcoming birthdays. They were exactly two weeks apart, and we usually celebrated them together. Momma said that this year we could have separate parties.

I spent weeks scrolling through magazines, looking for the perfect theme. I decided to go with a baseball card party. After all, cards were my first true love. I raved at the idea of receiving several packs of rare cards from all of my friends' parents. I skipped into the living room to share my bright idea with Momma when I noticed her pleading on the phone.

"Please, Mr. Kincaid, I need this job. If you lay me off, how am I going to provide for my kids?"

Hearing Momma practically beg for her job sent an eerie feeling through my body. I snuck back into my room, not truly understanding the magnitude of the conversation. After hearing her thrash the phone against the floor, I peeked out from behind my bedroom door. She was pacing along the living room smoking a cigarette. Ashes fell onto the floor as her hands shook and sadness covered her face. I had a strong feeling that drastic changes were on the way.

●●●

"So, it seems like Brookfield was the highlight of your childhood... Is that safe to say?"

"Yeah, Brookfield was everything to me. It's actually one of the highlights of my life to this very day. I just hate that it got cut so short."

"I'm assuming you're referring to the phone call your mom had with her boss. That seems like a very vivid memory for you. Why so?"

"Shit, because she got fired... And right after that,

we moved."

"And you think your Auntie Tika played a role in all of this?"

"Think? I know she did... Not about the whole getting fired thing, but I guarantee Momma being so ready to move had everything to do with Auntie Tika."

Dr. Bishop documented my response. "Deshaun, I honestly don't think you're giving your mom enough credit. Correct me if I'm wrong, but it seems as if you've placed a lot of her blame onto your aunt... I don't want you to take my observation the wrong way. I just thought I'd bring it to your attention."

"They both were out of line for a whole lot of shit. Either way, the shit was wrong."

"You're absolutely right... And you have every right to feel how you do." Dr. Bishop cracked a smile. "Can you finish telling me what happened after your mom received that unfortunate phone call?"

"Shit, I'd say a couple weeks later, Tiffany and me were on our way to the airport with one-way tickets to Nashville."

"Why didn't your mom go too?"

"She stayed back to tie up all her loose ends and ended up driving a U-Haul down with all of our stuff."

"That must've been horrific for you... Leaving your safe haven, Brookfield, and having to fly to a strange place to pretty much face your abuser all over again."

"The shit was terrible from the very beginning..."

● ● ●

Tiffany and I made the four-hour flight, mostly in silence. We'd been on a plane before, but never by ourselves. I sat in the aisle seat, staring at every person who crept to the bathroom. The airline escort occupied the middle seat. And Tiffany just swung her little legs back and forth, calmly peering out of the window ever so often. I obviously was taking our abrupt relocation the hardest.

But then again, Tiffany never seemed rattled. So, it wasn't a surprise to see her going with the flow.

I can still remember the scorching, dry, summer-time heat, and the smell of cow manure attacking my nose as soon as we exited the plane. Auntie Tika, Bobby Ray Jr., and the country ass pedophile, Bobby Ray, met us at baggage claim. It was my first time seeing him since I'd told on him.

My panic level spiked as he approached me with those same dingy eyes and rotten teeth. "Hey man, was the flight good?"

I stared at him in hatred. I couldn't believe that he was speaking to me as if nothing had ever happened. My miniature mean-mug was cut short when I felt a slap upside my head.

"Speak boy... I know you hear yo' uncle talking to you," said Auntie Tika, after palming the back of my freshly cut, bald fade.

At that moment, it became clear that I was on his home turf and Auntie Tika was his number one ally.

I rubbed my stinging head while speaking, "Hey, Uncle Bobby Ray."

Auntie Tika added insult to injury. "That's more like it. Now grab one of these bags and let's go."

Bobby Ray giggled and grabbed the other bag. The five of us headed for the exit. I lagged behind struggling with the oversized suitcase. It still smelled like Oakland. As a matter of fact, it smelled just like my room. I inhaled deeply, hoping that the scent of the bag would teleport Tiffany and me back to Brookfield. Sadly, that wasn't the case. Instead, we all climbed into an old white and wood-grain colored station wagon. It was dirty and crusty just like Bobby Ray. The seats were torn and covered in burn marks. If I had to guess what air freshener it smelled like, "Ashtray", would be my first choice. I snapped my seatbelt and looked at Tiffany. She was already gazing out of the window. There were times when I wished I could see what things looked like from her point of view. This day was definitely one of those times.

After a thirty-minute drive, we arrived at a run-down apartment complex. The entrance sign read "Haynes Manor." Each building was made of brick and went two stories up to form a four-plex. I couldn't help but notice the garbage dumpsters stacked to the top with trash as we navigated through the facility. Although it was dark, groups of people frolicked around the various buildings. It took at least 15 minutes of driving through the massive complex before we arrived at Auntie Tika's parking stall.

We entered the apartment and were immediately greeted by the biggest roach I'd ever seen. There were many other roaches that scattered once the lights flickered on. But this one in particular stood out. He was so huge that his wings made a flapping noise as he flew away.

As tough as Tiffany was, this was a different experience. She screamed and decided to jump onto me of all people.

Auntie Tika hollered out from the side of her mouth, while balancing a GPC menthol filter king cigarette between her lips, "Girl, hush… Them roaches ain't thinkin' 'bout you."

The three-piece microfiber furniture set located in the living room was raggedy, soiled, and reeked of tobacco. Cheap, out-of-date pictures of panthers and lions aligned the walls. On the coffee table was a picture of Momma, Tiffany, Bobby Ray Jr. and me. We'd taken it a couple of days before Auntie Tika left Oakland. After looking closely, I noticed that my face was slightly scratched out. Something told me that it wasn't an accident.

Tiffany and I followed Auntie Tika into our designated room. Inside the tiny living quarters was a neatly made full-sized bed. There was also a miniature television with a VCR attached sitting on a black dresser, and a small lamp resting on an old Cherrywood nightstand. On the floor was a piss-stained mattress with a folded sheet next to it and a pillow that'd seen better days. It looked like something she'd dragged in from the side of one of those overfilled dumpsters.

"Deshaun, let ya sister have the bed. You're a big boy, you'll be okay on the floor." Auntie Tika sprinkled baby powder around both Tiffany's bed and my heavily smudged mattress. She explained that it was a method to keep the roaches away. *But what about the flying one?* I thought to myself.

"My head hurts, I'm going to lay down... Let Bobby Ray know if y'all need something." Auntie Tika dragged into the hallway, leaving a poof of smoke in the air, and a trail of ashes on the dirty hardwood floor.

I didn't even bother to make the mattress up or even change my clothes for that matter. I curled up in the fetal position, stared at the ceiling, and waited for Tiffany to fall asleep so I could cry in peace.

● ● ●

"I can only imagine how vulnerable and afraid you must've felt. How were you able to cope until your mother arrived?"

"Prayer... I probably prayed a thousand times a day."

"Interesting, are you still a believer in prayer?"

"Not really... I gave up on that shit years ago."

"Can I ask you why?"

"Because if prayer was so powerful, I wouldn't have had to deal with all the fucked-up shit I'm dealing with now."

Dr. Bishop went back to recording in her notes. "Do you still believe in God?"

I thought long and hard before replying, "I don't know."

She eyed me in a way that a loving mother would a son. "How long did it take for your mom to get there?"

● ● ●

It seemed like forever and a day before Momma got to Nashville. Twenty-three days to be exact. Earlier that morning she'd called from a pay phone, notifying us that she was less than ten hours out. We were overly excited to hear the good news. Tiffany and I anxiously waited on the front porch, staring into every vehicle that even slightly resembled a moving truck.

Once the big U-Haul finally pulled into the parking lot, we raced to it as fast as we could. I was so excited to see her face. Although she was visibly exhausted, there was no question that she was happy to see us too.

"I missed y'all so so much... Where's your auntie?" asked Momma, while doing her best to show affection.

"In the house cooking," I replied.

Momma scrunched her face but didn't say anything.

After a long embrace, we lead her into Auntie Tika's apartment. Momma's confused expression gave me the impression that it wasn't what she expected.

"What the fuck is this?" mumbled Momma in disbelief.

I was actually relieved to hear her say that. Deep down, I knew Momma couldn't have signed us up to live in that dump. I wanted to warn her over the phone but Auntie Tika and Bobby Ray were monitoring our conversations closely like the FBI. Beyond that, I didn't necessarily feel comfortable saying too much after how my situation with Bobby Ray had panned out.

Tiffany and I guided her into the kitchen where Auntie Tika was cooking a pot of gumbo.

"Heeeeyyy twin, you finally made it."

Momma grabbed her by the arm and forced her out of the back door. The two had a bitter exchange of words resulting in Momma pushing her into the screen door. Auntie Tika backpedaled down the short stoop. Momma's raging adrenaline turned her pretty complexion to bloodshot red. She marched into the kitchen, signaled for Tiffany and me. "Grab y'all shit and let's go," and proceeded back towards the U-Haul. A part of me felt bad for Auntie

Tika. The other part of me was happy with the slice of karma she'd been fed.

I would soon find out that she misled Momma to believe that she'd lived in a spacious four-bedroom house located on a beautiful, fourteen-acre property, owned by Bobby Ray's parents. She'd even convinced Momma that it was plenty space to store our old furniture until her Section 8 was transferred over. What really made shit crazy, was that Auntie Tika provided Momma with pictures to support these lies. Come to find out, the photos were actually of a farmhouse belonging to Bobby Ray's brother-in-law. Auntie Tika had conveniently snapped the flicks with her Polaroid during a prior Thanksgiving gathering.

To make matters worse, Momma thought that we were only in the projects visiting Auntie Tika's friend. She was under the impression she was only stopping by to kiss her kids and grab the guesthouse keys from Auntie Tika so she could go get some much-needed rest. To say that she was hot would be an understatement.

Momma burnt rubber as she made her way out of the complex. Tiffany and I braced ourselves in silence. I turned to Momma just in time to see her tears forming. The gamble on Nashville had bitten her in the ass.

● ● ●

"Where'd you all go?" asked Dr. Bishop.

"To a hotel not far from the apartment complex... We stayed there for a few days and went back to Auntie Tika's house."

"Had you ever seen that side of your mom before?"

"I mean, I'd seen her mad, but never like that... Honestly, she never was the same after that day."

"Can you explain what you mean by that?'

"She seemed defeated. Prior to that, I'd only known her as a confident, strong, independent woman. Even in the midst of her partying, she'd maintained that status.

100

But I think betting on Nashville and crapping out depleted the little bit of fight she had left. Shit went downhill from there."

Dr. Bishop's wrist had to be getting tired from all of the writing she was doing. "So, once you all went back to your aunt's apartment how did things play out?"

"Let's just say a bad dream turned into a nightmare."

● ● ●

Momma took a turn for the worse once we went back to Auntie Tika's place. It was like a repeat of 69th Village times ten. She, Auntie Tika, and Bobby Ray partied from sunup to sundown. I still remember the loopy, chinky-eyed look she made whenever she was high. It reminded me of a dancer in the Michael Jackson Thriller video.

A fourth member joined the party soon after. His name was Junebug. Junebug was Bobby Ray's cousin. He was a big, muscular, country bumpkin, with the worst case of rotten teeth. Junebug was the epitome of an alcoholic. There was never a moment that I didn't see him clutching a pint-sized bottle of Seagram's Gin.

Momma and Junebug soon became a couple. Watching him kiss Momma with those tiny, brown, Chiclet-shaped teeth, made my stomach turn. They pranced around daily like two innocent love birds, flying high on a cloud of crack smoke.

That wasn't the case for Auntie Tika and Bobby Ray. They argued and bickered about any and everything. It seemed like every other night Bobby Ray was beating her upside the head. Momma tried to intervene, but Auntie Tika would somehow flip the blame as if it was her own fault.

Junebug wasn't much help. Bobby Ray often took his frustrations out on him with little resistance in return. At any given moment, he'd punch Junebug as a reminder of who was in charge. I never understood how a man with so many muscles could be such a coward. It was a sad sight to see this little man imposing his will on a giant like Junebug. It was like Evander Holyfield being bullied by Martin Lawrence with a Jheri curl.

● ● ●

"So, I take it you weren't too fond of Junebug?"

"I really didn't have a problem with him. I just didn't want him with Momma."

"Why not? Sounds like she was happy."

"She deserved better. Momma was way too pretty to be with a snaggletooth hillbilly like Junebug."

Dr. Bishop glanced at the wall clock. "Deshaun, sometimes we tend to want more for our loved ones than they want for themselves... And other times, we think our loved ones deserve more than what they actually do."

Her statement resonated with me deeply. "Man, you just don't know how real that shit is."

"I want you to consider the violence within the home, and how those events play a factor in the behavior you exhibit in your present life." She stood up. "But we'll save that for next session. We've already gone twenty minutes over. Have a wonderful week."

THERAPY SESSION #8

My palms and armpits perspired as I barged into Dr. Bishop's office. I'd barely eaten or slept in three days and my nerves were fried. I'd been pondering the suggestion she'd given me the week prior. Her exact words were, 'I want you to consider the violence within the home and how those events play a factor in the behavior you exhibit in your present life'. There was a specific, violent event that trumped everything I'd ever been through. She uncovered a lot about my life during our sessions, but this was a significant event I'd never told a single soul about. The countless nightmares that plagued me for years had done a number on my conscience. The guilt from this horrendous act had almost driven me to the brink of suicide.

Dr. Bishop was at her desk doing prep work when I barged in and took a seat.

I removed my North Face jacket and fanned my shirt, trying my best to cool off. My knees trembled so hard against each other they made a clanking sound.

Dr. Bishop with her eyebrows contorted, tilted her head, and zoned in on my demeanor. She removed a bottle of water from the fridge and slowly brought it over to me.

I twisted the cap off and guzzled the entire bottle in three gulps.

"Breathe Deshaun—breathe," she repeated.

I shut my eyes, breathed, and did my best to block out any thoughts. After a few minutes of meditation, I opened them.

"What's on your mind?" asked Dr. Bishop softly.

I swayed back and forth, biting my nails while staring at the floor. "You might want to get your pen and pad out."

Dr. Bishop hustled to her desk, retrieved her writing materials, and quickly returned to my side. "Okay, I'm all ears whenever you're ready."

● ● ●

The most traumatic thing I'd ever experienced happened around the time Momma got with Junebug. A couple months passed and the nighttime festivities were now the norm. The party crew would be calling it quits right before it was time for Tiffany and me to get up and get ready for school. It's funny how the music going off served as our signal to get dressed.

Auntie Tika would often be the last one up, barely keeping her eyes open long enough to fix Bobby Ray Jr.'s breakfast. I never knew how she was able to party all night and still stay woke long enough to care for a toddler. Auntie Tika got so good at balancing the two that she decided to take on another child.

The next-door neighbor, Sicily, was a single mother in her early twenties who, like us, didn't have any family in the area. She worked the morning shift at the local hospital and desperately needed a babysitter. For some odd reason, Sicily thought Auntie Tika was the perfect candidate. Her son, Dontay, was around the same age as Bobby Ray Jr. so I could see why she thought it'd be a good idea.

Dontay was a quiet little boy. Every morning, he'd sit in front of the television without making a sound. I found it a little odd for a three-year-old, seeing that, Bobby Ray Jr. couldn't sit still. He jumped all over the place from the time he woke up 'til the time he went to sleep. Dontay was the complete opposite.

A couple of weeks passed when I noticed something different. Dontay would run to me every morning before I left for school. He'd cling on to me so tightly that I'd barely be able to peel him off. When I did manage to hand him over to Auntie Tika, he'd holler at the top of his lungs. The frantic cries from those tiny little lungs still haunt me to this day.

Shortly after, lumps and contusions appeared on Dontay's body. One morning, I even noticed that he had a busted lip. When Tiffany and I returned from school that day, we overheard Auntie Tika explaining to Sicily that Dontay had hit his lip on the corner of a coffee table. I could see the skepticism is Sicily's eyes. Still, Dontay was right back over the very next morning.

After that day, I started paying closer attention to the way Auntie Tika handled Dontay. The results of that observation were horrifying. I secretly watched her shove spoons down his throat until he choked, slap him across the head until his gentle little body stiffened, pinch his thigh until he helplessly screamed, and coach Bobby Ray Jr. into jabbing him like a living punching bag. I couldn't believe that she was abusing this precious little boy. The evil look in her eyes was cold, dark, and blank whenever she did it.

All I could think about was how vulnerable Dontay must've felt. This small, delicate, baby boy was being a-bused by the woman his mother trusted with his life. I didn't understand how Momma and Junebug allowed this to go on. But then again, it's hard to hear anything when you're in a drunken slumber. For all I knew, Bobby Ray's bitch-ass was a part of the whole thing.

A part of me wanted to tell someone—a teacher, principal, police officer, even Momma maybe. But then I remembered what happened the last time I opened my big mouth to one of those trusted few. Telling the truth hadn't gotten me very far at all. If anything, it only made things worse. So, against my better judgement, I kept my mouth shut.

It was a Friday and I'd just gotten home from school. Auntie Tika, Bobby Ray, Bobby Ray Jr., and Dontay were all in the living room. Sicily was off on Fridays, so it was unusual to see Dontay over on that day. Come to find out, she'd gone out of town to Atlanta with a group of friends for Freaknik. That left Dontay in Auntie Tika's care for the entire weekend—huge mistake. I spoke to everyone and went upstairs to hang up my coat and backpack. Feeling a little parched, I headed back downstairs for a glass of Kool-Aid. On the way down, I heard Dontay's familiar screech. I paused in the middle of the stairway, hoping no one had seen me. As I crouched down to get a better look, I witnessed Auntie Tika repeatedly back slapping Dontay in the forehead. His eyes rolled back into his head. Bobby Ray just sat there staring at the television as if he hadn't seen anything. I was completely disgusted. It seemed like Auntie Tika's brazenness increased by the day. I positioned myself to get a better look.

Bobby Ray spotted me from the corner of his eye. "Get down here, boy."

Those next ten steps took forever.

When I made it downstairs, Auntie Tika pointed her finger and asked me, "What did you see, Deshaun?"

It was hard to hear over Dontay's screams of agony, but I managed to make out what she'd asked. I quickly responded with my head down, "Nothing, Tee Tee."

Bobby Ray stood and came towards me. "Boy, stop lying."

I peered up only to see his dingy eyes piercing through me. I was terrified of this man. Before I knew it, a confession left my mouth. "Okay, I saw you hit Dontay... But I promise I won't say anything."

Auntie Tika eyeballed me with the same possessed look she'd given Dontay just moments prior. "Baby, turn up the volume on the TV," she said to Bobby Ray.

My mind was bewildered about what was going to happen next. Bobby Ray followed her command without taking his rusty eyes off of me. Auntie Tika inched her way to the bottom of the stairs. She peeked up to make sure Momma and yuck mouth Junebug wasn't coming down. Next, she balled my shirt into her fist and shoved me towards Dontay. It was obvious her pinned-up frustration towards me had finally boiled over. My body shuddered as Bobby Ray removed his belt from the pair of ashy black Bugle Boy jeans he was wearing. The first step he took towards me was reminiscent of the day he'd molested me. I don't know who was more scared, me or Dontay.

Auntie Tika took one last glimpse towards the stairway and turned to me. "Hit 'em."

I stood there uncertain of what she was asking of me.

Auntie Tika beamed into my eyes, clamped me by the arm with her sharp, chipped nails, and dug deeply into my bicep. "I... said... hit... him."

Everything went into slow motion. I couldn't believe my auntie was asking me to hit a three-year-old. Dontay's head jerked in my direction as if he knew what was coming next. His cries became louder. I wanted to cry, too. Bobby Ray wrapped the belt around his fist and took another step forward. I was so terrified that before I knew it, I'd swung and landed a punch right to Dontay's temple. His teeny, little body froze like an ice cube.

Auntie Tika still wasn't satisfied. She lifted him up from the carpet, sunk her claws deeper into my arm, and stared even deeper into my soul. "Do it again."

I turned away, looking for a path to run upstairs, only to see Bobby Ray hovering closer. As I turned back in Dontay's direction, I could see him holding his face. This was a baby. How could anyone be so hateful to sink low enough to harm a child? Better yet, force another child to commit the crime?

My mind was cloudy. My heart was weak from beating so rapidly. The walls started closing in. The room was spinning. Sweat dribbled down my back. Drips of urine began to trickle down my leg. I tried to pray but Auntie Tika's grip was getting tighter, Bobby Ray's belt was getting closer, Dontay's screeches were getting stronger. *Momma please help*, was the only thing playing through my mind. But to no surprise, she was nowhere to be found in my darkest time. Auntie Tika's talons were now meat deep. After holding back for as long as I could, I finally succumbed to the insurmountable pressure. I clutched my left fist and did as instructed. Dontay was so dazed he didn't even cry.

My first thought was that I had killed him. I dropped to my knees, eyes balling, thinking I'd just murdered a baby with my bare hands.

Auntie Tika made sure to pour on additional guilt to my already grief-stricken pallet. "You see what you did? Nobody told you to hit him that hard... You better hope he's still alive or you're going to jail for murder."

Bobby Ray shook his dry curls up and down while slapping the belt against his left palm, further inciting my nervous breakdown.

My body twitched as I did my best to take in what was being said. All the while, poor little Dontay laid next to me motionless. The two cold-hearted demons cackled as they watched me panic. They knew that Dontay wasn't dead, and also that they had me right where they wanted.

Auntie Tika leaned down beside me, cuffed the lower part of my face, and whispered in a tone that mirrored my idea of Satan's voice, "If you mention this to yo' Momma, you know who she's believing... Now take yo' nosey, punk-ass back upstairs before I let Bobby Ray deal wit' you." She stood up and lifted me by the collar before slapping me upside the head.

I rubbed my stinging head and sidestepped Bobby Ray on my way upstairs. He gave me a slight nudge with his elbow before I steered clear. I was completely mortified. In my mind, I'd just committed the ultimate act of sin. Once again, I'd been violated at the expense of my own actions. I shuffled into the room, quietly shutting the door behind me. Tiffany sat on her bed, lost in the sounds of her handheld AM/FM radio, oblivious to what I'd just endured. I spread my shivering body onto the floor mattress and prayed for forgiveness until mental exhaustion forced me to sleep.

●●●

Dr. Bishop's eyes were as big as two tennis balls after the bombshell I'd just dropped on her. Yet, she did her best to keep a calm, professional demeanor. "Those were very disturbing details you just shared. The adults were totally wrong for what they did... You and baby Dontay were both victims to a cruel, unsafe environment. Now I have a better understanding of why you resent her so much."

It was my first time sharing that story with anyone. For twenty-three years, I carried that weight on my back like a ton of bricks.

My voice cracked as I wept my heart out. "I fuckin' hate her. She made me beat a three-year-old baby. The sound of him crying haunts me every... single... night. For years, I wanted to kill my fuckin' self."

Dr. Bishop slowly approached with a box of tissue. She extended her arms, pulled me in tightly, and warmly caressed my back. She held me for several minutes without saying a single word. I could feel her positive energy transferring into my damaged soul.

Dr. Bishop lifted my chin and dabbed my dreary eyes. "I want you to know that you're not responsible for the things that were forced on to you as a child. You were poorly misguided, and devilishly persuaded into doing things that would've broken anyone down... Today was a major step towards getting better." She smiled. "I'm so proud of you, Deshaun."

The last five words she uttered didn't get thrown my way much.

I'd sought validation my entire life only to be rejected and neglected by the persons who owed it to me the most. And here it was, this stranger, going over and beyond to lift my spirit out of darkness.

Dr. Bishop held me tighter. "Repeat after me—I'm proud of myself."

"I'm proud of myself," I repeated.

"I'm worthy of love just the way I am."

"I'm worthy of love just the way I am," I repeated.

"I will work diligently to get better."

"I will work diligently to get better."

"I will learn to forgive those who've wronged me."

I hesitated but didn't want to let Dr. Bishop down. "I will learn to forgive those who've wronged me."

"And most importantly, I'll learn to forgive myself."

"And most importantly, I'll learn to forgive myself."

She placed both hands on my shoulders. "Healing is like building a house. The foundation has to be firm before adding all the amenities. Forgiveness for yourself and others will be your fundament." She led me to her desk, reached into a drawer, and handed me a book. The small, compact, purple book with gold writing was titled, *Forgiveness: 21 Days to Forgive Everyone for Everything*, by Iyanla Vanzant. "Since we won't be seeing each other until after the holidays, I figured I'd give you a little practice work. Your assignment is to read this book in its entirety. There are daily messages, affirmations, and exercises inside that require you to log notes into a journal after each chapter. It even has a free audio download of meditation practices that I'm sure you'll find more than useful."

The stories of my childhood had been something I'd ran from for decades. Each terrible memory consumed my energy a huge chunk at a time. Still and all, I felt a sense of relief as I released that pressure off my shoulders. Sharing my shaky upbringing with Dr. Bishop allowed me to initiate the process of conquering the ignominy of my past.

I took another look at the book. Shamefully, I hadn't read one since college. Forgiveness was something I'd never been able to do. And there it was written boldly across the top. I knew deep down inside that I had to let go. The problem was I didn't know how. I know one thing, *Iyanla Vanzant better have the damn answers if I'mma read this whole fuckin' book*, is what I thought as I waved goodbye and wished her a happy holiday.

A slight smile formed on her face while watching me flip through the pages of the book on my way out. "Don't let the size fool you now. That book can be a powerful weapon if used properly."

THERAPY SESSION #9

After being away for three weeks, it felt different coming into Dr. Bishop's office. Crazy as it seemed, I actually missed the place. Having an unbiased set of ears to vent to was slowly becoming something I looked forward to.

Unfortunately, it would be my last session before judgement day. A week prior, I'd gone to my court hearing and desperately needed to talk to Dr. Bishop. In the three months since my initial court date, I'd only spoken to my court-appointed attorney once. He informed me that the prosecutor offered a deal of thirty-six to sixty months, but a whole lot more time was on the table if I decided to take it to trial. Three to five years in prison wasn't something I was trying to hear. But the risk of losing the case and getting the maximum of eighty-four months scared the living daylights out of me. The frightening thing about it was I only had thirty days to accept the offer or it would be removed from the table.

On top of that, I still had the restriction of not being able to see or talk to my babies. That stressed me out more than anything. I know I wasn't the best father in the world, but I definitely loved my children. God knows I would've given anything in the world to hug and kiss on them during that crucial time. Needless to say, I had a lot on my mind as I entered Dr. Bishop's healing sanctuary.

"Mr. Nelson, it's great to see you. Welcome back."

"What's up, Doc?" I took position on my favorite end of the couch. "How are you?"

"I'm blessed. Thanks for asking. How have things been since we last met?"

"It's been—ehhh."

"Ehhh, huh? You care to explain?"

"I went to court last week, and they offered me thirty-six to sixty months."

"How much time are you looking at if you don't take it?" asked Dr. Bishop

"It's eighty-four months if I lose the trial."

She took a deep breath. "It's easy for me to sit here and give advice on what I think you should or shouldn't do, but if all fails, you're the one who has to serve the time. What I will say is nothing is ever as bad as it seems. It's always worse in the moment. But in hindsight, it's just a small bump in the long road of life. You're young, intelligent, with a full life ahead of you. Whatever you decide to do, just make sure you're at peace with it."

"How can I be at peace when I know either way I'm going to prison?"

"Well—let me ask you this, and be honest with me... Did you commit the crimes you've been accused of?"

"Yeah, I did," I mumbled.

"I know you may not want to hear this, but if you dug the hole, then you're the one who has to dig your way out of it. And as harsh as it may sound, taking responsibility for your actions is the only way to make the situation better. Now, it may very well cost you some time away, but—you'll come out on the other side of this a better man, as long as you accept accountability."

Accepting prison was going to be a hard pill to swallow. "Your recommendation is going to help at sentencing, right?"

"It might. I can't make any promises though. The

judge can either take it into consideration or reject it. But what I can tell you, had you not come in here and participated, the final report would've certainly worked against you."

All I could do was shake my head. As bad as I didn't want to accept it, Dr. Bishop was right. There wasn't anyone else to blame other than myself. I'd created this dilemma, and it was up to me to figure it out.

"I know it's easier said than done but try not to stress over things you don't have any control over. The most important thing is getting better so you don't repeat or compound the consequences."

"Listen, you don't have to worry about me doing any dumb shit like that anymore. I, for sure, learned my lesson."

"Lessons are always a blessing, Deshaun. This unfortunate circumstance might just be exactly what you needed to flourish as a man."

"Yeah, you're right."

Dr. Bishop placed her hand behind her ear before blurting out a caustic remark, "Whoa, whoa, whoa—did you just say I was right? Is that what I just heard?"

I couldn't fight back the smile. "Yeah, you heard right. Don't push it, though."

"Un uh, it took me months to get that out of you. I'm gon' push it."

We both shared a laugh.

"So, I see you brought the book. Did you do your homework?" she asked like a 10th-grade geometry teacher.

I grabbed the book, waving it side to side. "Yes, Mrs. Bishop," I said in a playful, third-grader tone.

"Wonderful, so what'd you think?"

"I actually thought it was pretty dope. I gained a lot of insight and really liked the way she used her own experiences in each chapter to help resonate the message."

Dr. Bishop's eyes beamed with delight as she sat on the top of her desk. "I'm so happy to hear you say that.

You know what was pretty dope? The way you opened up last session. It doesn't get any doper than that if you ask me."

Her kind words were dope in itself. Now, her overly proper use of the word could've used a little help.

I chuckled a little before responding, "Thanks."

"No—thank you..." Her Chi-town slang randomly reappeared. "Now, about my play auntie, Iyanla. Ain't she good? I swear she's like the mentor I've never had. I want to be just like her when I grow up," she joked with a grin as wide as the room. "Tell me, what did you like most about the book?"

By the excitement in her tone, I could definitely tell she was a huge fan.

"I'd probably have to say the way each day represented a different thing to forgive. You know, how day one was to forgive myself and day two was to forgive my body. I really liked that about the book."

"Wasn't that brilliant of her?" she asked.

Dr. Bishop had two identical sheets of paper in her hand. She handed me one before finally taking a seat. "So, today we're going to do a couple of exercises similar to the book but with a slight spin. I'll start with a sequence of statements, you'll fill in the blank, and we'll briefly discuss the answers after all the statements have been concluded." She pulled her patented stare-over-the-eyeglasses look. "I'm warning you now though, I'm going to be prying pretty deep so get prepared."

"Yeah, that's coo'," I responded, not knowing exactly what was coming next.

"All right, statement number one... I forgive myself for..."

My synopsis fired off quicker than I'd expected. "Believing that I'm a failure."

"I forgive my mind for..."

"Thinking I was to blame for being molested."

"I forgive my body for..."

"The abuse it's endured by the hands of my of-

116

fenders."

"I forgive my soul for..."

"Questioning whether I should end my life."

The acceptance of responsibility in my answers must've caught her by surprise.

Dr. Bishop stopped writing and mustered up a huge smile. "It takes an immense amount of bravery to forgive—which is why I started with statements of forgiving yourself. Self-forgiveness is the gateway to forgiving others, which leads to understanding that everything is exactly the way it needs to be in order for you to blossom into your full potential. Every single wrong you've committed thus far presents an opportunity to grow, learn, and become wiser—no matter how serious or unforgiveable the offense may seem." She peeked at the paper. "My heart filled with joy when you mentioned forgiving yourself for being molested. Tell me how that came about."

I opened the book and turned the pages until I landed on page forty-eight. "So, as I was reading, I ran across this prayer called, A Prayer of Forgiveness. It goes, 'Today, I ask for and open myself to receive the strength, courage, and compassion required to forgive myself. I forgive myself for all perceived sins, faults, mistakes, and failings. I forgive myself for every thought, belief, behavior, perception, and emotion that I have told myself is bad, wrong, unjust, unloving, and displeasing to You, God. I forgive myself for every hurt, judgement, condemnation, unkind or unloving thought, belief, and perception I have held about or against myself. I forgive myself for any behaviors, habits, or actions motivated by unforgiveness, the unwillingness to forgive myself. I forgive myself with compassion and love. I ask for, accept, and claim God's forgiveness. Today, believing and knowing that because I have asked, I have received. I am so grateful. I let it be! And so, it is!' I recited it every day until I started to memorize it. The more I read it the more I understood the importance of giving myself another chance. I can't control what the judge decides but I can work towards dictating a better future for myself. That part starts from within."

"Spoken like a true king," said Dr. Bishop with a proud nod of gratitude.

She focused her attention back to the paper. "Unfortunately, for every forgivable act, there's usually an act or two we just aren't quite able to give in to yet. And that's okay because we're only human. However, acknowledgement is the first step to correction... I'm going to ask you another series of questions. Fill in the blank same as before... I'm not quite ready to forgive myself for..."

"Being in the fucked-up predicament that I'm in now."

"I'm not quite ready to forgive my mind for..."

I paused. "Thinking it was okay to put my hands on Eve and Trina."

"I'm not quite ready to forgive my body for..."

"Fiending for the drugs that always seem to get me in trouble."

"I'm not quite ready to forgive my soul for..."

I paused even longer. "Abusing Dontay."

"Some things take longer to forgive than others. Don't feel bad because it happens to everyone. The key is to continue to do the necessary work to eventually let go of everything. For some, that can be a lifelong journey. With that being said, it's important that we take it not one day, but one situation at a time, seeing that multiple situations can occur in a single day." She delayed her response and softened her voice, "The thing I need you to forgive yourself for more than anything is the Dontay situation. That burden isn't yours to carry. If anything, you were a victim just like he was a victim."

My throat crinkled making it almost impossible to swallow. "So why does it hurt so badly?"

"Any person who'd experienced something like that would suffer the same guilt. Your compassion is a testament to the character buried beneath all that baggage you've been carrying. I'm here to tell you that burden isn't yours, Deshaun. That belongs to the adults who forced you to do it. They have to make peace with that—not you."

I raised my head, spotting her smiling my way.

"One thing I'm extremely proud of is the accountability in regard to your treatment of both Eve and Trina. Just a couple of months ago, you were poking your chest out boasting about using physical abuse to put them in their places. So, to hear you show remorse in regard to that is a huge deal. What exactly shifted your mindset?"

"I can't forgive myself for something I refuse to own up to—which also means I can't get better unless I address it. It was time to finally look myself in the mirror and man up."

Dr. Bishop removed her glasses and twirled them. "Okay—hold up. Who are you? And what did you do with Deshaun?"

I laughed at her sarcasm. "I'm right here, Doc. Just trying to be better and make sense of all the turmoil in my life."

"Look how far you've come. Not too long ago I thought I was going to have to clunk you upside your big ol' bald head for how you were cutting up in here. Now, you're owning up and accepting responsibility like a true man of valor. I can't tell you enough how proud I am."

"Thanks, Doc. That means a lot."

"You're absolutely welcome." She smiled before continuing, "This next sequence of questions is going to be about making amends. Forgiveness and apology go hand in hand. Together, they form a strong blade that can cut through any amount of built up trauma. Apologies can be tricky though. Feelings aren't facts, they're someone's reality. Therefore, we don't get to dictate when or if they decide to accept the apology. It is merely a way of showing remorse and extending the opportunity for them to accept it. But what it does for the individual, in this case you, is allow the chance to release shame, guilt, and a gigantic load from your shoulders... The first person you owe an apology to is yourself. So, let's start there. I apologize to myself for..."

"Not living up to my true potential."

She sat upright before intervening, "You'd be surprised how many people feel they've fallen short of their purpose. We all tend to have a certain expectation of how our lives are supposed to pan out. But that's the thing... We have a plan—then God has a different one. And whose do you think will prevail in the end?"

"God's."

"Exactly, and everything He's allowed you to go through to this point is all in accordance with His ultimate purpose over your life. You just have to trust the process." Dr. Bishop wagged her finger at me. "What you're doing in this very moment is going to make that process a whole lot easier. Just have faith."

"I'm trying."

"And you're doing an excellent job," said Dr. Bishop before continuing. "The next statement is—I apologize to Eve for..."

"All the shit I've put her through over the years."

"I apologize to Trina for..."

Several moments passed as I replayed the complexity of me and Trina's entanglement. I'd treated her with so much disrespect that it was difficult to narrow down just one thing to apologize for.

"Take your time," whispered Dr. Bishop.

"Misleading her," I responded shortly after.

"Why the hesitation?"

"Because there were so many instances that I should apologize for, it was hard to pick just one."

"I'm curious to know why you didn't use that same logic when it came to apologizing to Eve?"

"The thing is, I loved Eve and had every intention of spending the rest of my life with her. Although things imploded towards the end, we still had many successful years together. I can't say the same for Trina. Our situationship was built on lies and false pretense. I strung her along for so long, giving the impression that it would be just me and her in the end. So, picking one thing to apologize for was more difficult."

"Okay, now I get it... Speaking of Trina—did the results come back yet?"

"They did." I said while rubbing my clean-shaven head.

"And?" she asked anxiously.

"He's ninety-nine-point-nine-nine-nine-eight percent—mine."

She stood and applauded like I'd won a Grammy, "Congratulations."

"Thanks—I guess."

"Have you spoken with Trina?"

"No, I haven't reached out yet."

"Well, now that the paternity has been confirmed, don't you think you should go see your son."

I swiftly cut her off. "No disrespect, but I'm not there yet. I still need time to process everything."

"Proper preparation prevents poor performance, so I won't press the issue. I'm more than confident you'll do the right thing," said Dr. Bishop as she scampered to her desk. She grabbed a few sheets of lined paper and a pen.

"For our next exercise, I'd like to focus on the power of releasing. It's crucial that we unclench the grip that binds unhealthy attachments. In this instance, your magnetic attachments are a direct correlation with people—the ones who've either hurt you or who you've hurt. In order to move forward in your healing, these attachments must be broken." She set her sights on the wall clock. "Take the next thirty minutes or so to write letters to the three people that've hurt you most. I think we both know exactly who they are. It doesn't have to be a certain word count like in college, however, be sure to cover how they hurt you and if you're able to forgive them or not. If you're not quite able to release, don't feel bad. Just write down whatever it is you feel."

"You're really about to make me do this, huh?"

"Trust me, I wouldn't have asked if I didn't feel you were ready."

I closed my eyes and bowed my head. Not necessarily to pray—but to fully digest her request.

The three people who'd hurt me most were the only ones who'd ever hurt me my entire life. Anyone else didn't get an opportunity to do so. And if they did, I deliberately hurt them before they even came close. That's how emotionnally detached I had become over the years.

Decades of harboring resentment towards those three individuals subsequently turned me into a completely different person. Was that the way I wanted my kids to view me? Was that what I wanted my sons to emulate? Was that what I wanted my daughter to marry?

Those were the questions that gave me enough motivation to attempt forgiveness. The only way to prevent those things from happening was to try my best to push forward into a new way of thinking and living. My worst nightmare would be inflicting the same trauma on to them that for so long dwelled inside of me.

I tapped the back of the pen against the paper that was supported by a clear, plastic clipboard.

"No rush. Just let me know when you're ready," murmured Dr. Bishop.

My hands began to shake.

"Breathe, Deshaun. Breathe," she said.

I closed my eyes and did the STAR technique she'd taught me a while back. After a minute of centering myself, I let my heart, mind, and pen go to work.

The thirty-minute timer sounded off as I inked the last few words of the last letter.

"Okay, times up. How do you feel?"

"I feel okay," I said after a deep gasp.

Dr. Bishop retrieved three stamped envelopes and an empty Folgers coffee tin can and placed them on the floor between us.

"What are those for?"

"Releasing is not about the other person, it's about you. However, in some cases it's therapeutic to let the individuals who've wronged you know exactly how you feel. That decision is completely up to you. Today you have two options. Either you can mail each letter to the intended person or we can burn them in the can after reading them aloud."

I reached into my pocket and grabbed a lighter. "I don't even need to read them out loud. We can burn that shit right now."

"Wait a second. That's not the way it works. The reasoning for reading each letter out loud is to release the emotion into the atmosphere. You need to feel and hear in order to bring as much closure as possible."

I rocked back and forth while staring into the distance. A panic attack was brewing.

Dr. Bishop came and knelt beside me. "Breathe. You're not alone. Breathe. I'm right here with you."

I held her hand tightly as air slowly seeped between my partially closed lips, slowly breathing in and out.

"Are you okay?" she calmly asked.

I slowly nodded yes.

"Would you like more time before going forward?"

"Nah, I'm okay."

"Well, I'm staying right here just in case."

Having her there beside me gave me a boost of confidence. I cleared my throat, sat up straight, and read aloud,

"Bobby Ray, my innocence and purity were snatched away when you committed that despicable crime against me. I spent my entire childhood blaming myself for what you did. For years, I questioned whether what happened made me queer or not. The psychological damage you've caused has given me decades of insecurity.

"Today, I've decided to release my resentment towards you. Not because you deserve it. But because I no longer want to give your disgusting act power over my life. I want to be free in my thoughts and actions. In order to do that, I must start the process of forgiveness. Although I'm not quite able to forgive you at this moment, I'll be diligently striving to lift off layers of that weight one day at a time."

I immediately balled the letter up and tossed it into the tin can.

Dr. Bishop rubbed my back in a circular motion. "That was brave, powerful, and perfectly articulated. Let me remind you that releasing those feelings had nothing to do with him and everything to do with you letting go. I'm proud of you."

I did my best not to choke up as I read the next letter,

"Auntie Tika, the things you forced me to do to Dontay were absurd, cruel, and vicious. There isn't a day that passes by that I don't think about the harm I caused that precious, innocent little boy. On many nights, I've awakened in cold sweats panicking over the way you coaxed me into abusing him. It even got so bad that I contemplated taking my own life. I trusted you like a second mother. And you used that influence to direct me into an act that has haunted me my whole life.

"However, I'm learning to forgive you. Why? Because in order to seek forgiveness for the harm I've done to others, I must first learn how to release the grudges I harbor towards the ones who've hurt me."

I ripped the paper into tiny pieces before dumping them in the can.

Dr. Bishop remained beside me nobly smiling as I grabbed the last letter. "Take a deep breath. You're doing great."

The last letter was made out to the person who'd hurt me the worst.

"Momma, I love you with all of my heart. But there are things I've resented you for my entire life. There were moments when I felt abandoned, unprotected, unwanted, and even unloved. Your battles with addiction, depression, and instability inadvertently created an unsafe environment that brought me extreme anguish as a child. My current struggle with accountability is a direct reflection of what you've shown throughout the years. All of the years we lived on government assistance made me feel inferior. You providing the bare minimum caused insecurities that made me feel unconfident throughout my entire adolescence. Although this letter may seem harsh, it's my reality. These are feelings that your actions have created. But I'm not writing this letter to bash you. It's actually intended to forgive you. In order to let go, I had to let out. And since you've never been able to give me a platform to express my feelings, this was the only option.

"As I journey into healing, I realize we're more similar than I thought. We both abuse substances as a way of running from the things we aren't able to change, only digging a deeper hole of guilt and self-hatred. We both try to sleep away the day hoping that the depression that greets us 'good morning' will wear off with a couple more hours of shut eye. We both inflict pain on others with a mirror mentality because of how low we think of ourselves. And worst of all, we both have let down the people who rely on our mental stability the most—our children.

"Through therapy, I've learned that the first step to correction is acknowledgment. But I've also learned that the very next step is forgiveness. And because I'm able to acknowledge the fact that life doesn't come with a handbook on how to be a parent, I'm able to take the necessary steps to forgive you for the areas you fell short in. I can no longer spend my life blaming you for things that I'm now doing myself. Instead, I'm going to release any ill will and bitterness, offering you a clean slate. I hope that you receive and take advantage of the opportunity. If not, I'll forgive you for that as well."

A wave of emotion knocked me into a sea of cries. My hands jittered as I folded the letter in half and placed it into one of the envelopes.

Dr. Bishop pulled me in close. "That's right, release it."

Several minutes passed with me in her arms. I could hear her sniffling away tears of her own.

"That was truly amazing. The eloquence penned in

that letter was superb, to say the least. Understanding the power of forgiveness is one of the most important keys of obtaining the peace of mind that we all desire to have."

I pulled the lighter out from my pocket. "I'm ready to be done with this shit."

She passed me the metal coffee can. "Go ahead and do the honors."

I watched closely as the fire slowly burned. The longer it went, the higher the flames lifted.

Dr. Bishop took a cup of sand and poured it into the can. The flames receded and turned into white smoke. The fire or paper was no longer there. Only harmless ashes remained. At that moment, I understood the whole point of therapy. Trauma was like one big fire. It's hot, unbearable, and the longer it goes untreated, the stronger it becomes. But once you find enough courage to douse it, impotent ashes become the only thing left to deal with.

JUDGEMENT DAY

The day I'd been dreading had finally arrived. A week prior, my attorney notified me that I'd be taken into custody immediately following the judge's decision. Therefore, mentally I was somewhat prepared. It still didn't help my nerves any. They'd been shot more and more the closer it came to the day.

I agreed to take the thirty-six to sixty-month sentence that the District Attorney had offered, hoping Dr. Bishop's recommendation would secure the lesser. We tried to get the prosecutor to come down some, but I was sure being a woman representing the state in a domestic violence related case didn't play too well on her compassion for me. At the end of the day, I was wrong and had to answer for my poor decisions. Four months ago, I would've never admitted that. But my time with Dr. Bishop taught me a valuable lesson about owning up.

When I slipped inside of the court room, Dr. Bishop was the first person I saw. She, an attorney, and a client of hers were standing before the judge as she gave her recommendations. Apparently, he didn't embrace the therapy quite as well as I had, and the judge let him know his displeasure by sentencing him to the maximum.

"One hundred and twenty months," is what Judge

Bellingford said, sentenced him to without even making eye contact with the man. *Damn, a ten piece?* Is what went through my mind as the dispirited defendant slumped with his head down, while being dragged away by the deputy.

Case after case had identical outcomes. Minority men committing crimes and Judge Bellingford making them pay for it. My attorney briefly sat beside me to go over the upcoming procedure. His words fell on deaf ears, while sweat saturated the lining of my collared shirt as my turn approached.

Dr. Bishop noticed me looking anxious and mouthed, "Deep breaths."

Moments later, the judge called my name, "The next case is the people versus Deshaun Nelson."

My attorney and I took our rightful places as the judge carefully looked over the plea agreement.

"Dr. Bishop, can you please read off your recommendation?" he asked.

She glanced at me before approaching the bench. "Deshaun Nelson is a young black man suffering from post-traumatic stress disorder. His troubled childhood consisted of extreme violence and many variations of abuse. Mr. Nelson is plagued by psychological shock and constantly reminded of negative experiences that have inadvertently dulled his conscience towards others. During our time of therapy, he's shown great strides of accepting this condition, and has made a commitment to living a healthier lifestyle. His engagement was exceptional, and his perfect attendance reflected the desire necessary to heal and move beyond his current circumstances. He's also shown genuine remorse towards the victims and has a deep passion to make things right. I recommend one year of inpatient rehabilitation treatment, extensive therapy, followed by supervised probation. As a father of three, I'm confident that he understands the severity of becoming a healthy, law-abiding citizen, and will take the proper steps to do so. I know it's not my decision to make, but I strongly oppose incarceration in this case."

"Thank you, Dr. Bishop," said Judge Bellingford. "Mr. Nelson, is there anything you'd like to say before I render my judgement?"

I held my chin high. "Your Honor, I take full responsibility for my actions and will respect whatever decision you choose to make."

Dr. Bishop relished like a parent whose child had taken its first steps.

Judge Bellingford took a long look at me. "It seems as though you've made a good impression on Dr. Bishop. In spite of that, I can't ignore the recklessness you displayed on that eventful night. People could've died due to your actions and that's something I just can't let go easily." He paused momentarily. "I'm not opposed to the inpatient rehabilitation, but only after you've paid your debt to society. Instead of the thirty-six to sixty-month plea agreement you signed, I'm sentencing you to twenty-four months in the California Department of Corrections, followed by a year of inpatient rehabilitation treatment. You'll also be placed on five-year felony parole once your term is completed. I hope you've learned a valuable lesson and intend on flying a straight path going forward. Case adjourned."

Dr. Bishop rested both hands against her cheeks and muttered, "I'm so sorry."

I winked and smiled, letting her know that I wasn't disappointed. To be honest, I was actually at peace with the verdict. No longer was I willing to place blame on others. For the first time in my entire life, I'd fully accepted sole responsibility without deflecting blame on anyone else. I knew she was proud of the way I handled it. More importantly... I was proud of myself.

I began therapy as a ruthless, narcissistic, womanizer with zero regard for anyone outside of myself. Anytime life reminded me of my past shortcomings, I'd drown myself in alcohol and drugs. Therapy helped me realize that faulting others wasn't the answer to my problems. Actually, it was the very thing holding me back.

Tracing the origins of my trauma is what ultimately set me free. Digging deeply within to address internal wounds served as the blueprint to a healthier future. Did nine sessions with a psychiatrist deem me as cured? Absolutely not. My healing journey had actually just begun. Be that as it may, I was something I'd never been before— enlightened, aware, and accountable. And sometimes a sample of what you've never known, is just enough to pursue the things you've always needed.

ONE YEAR LATER...

Dear Dr. Bishop,

How are things going out there? Good, I hope. I'd first like to start off by thanking you for everything. The tools and techniques you've given me have done wonders for my life. Without you, I don't know where I'd be. Well, I'd be locked up either way, but you get the point. So much taboo has been placed on therapy within the black community, and as a result, our entire race is deprived of the healing we so desperately need.

Thanks to you, there isn't a day that goes by that I don't work towards becoming a better overall human being. Typically, prison isn't the ideal place to do so but I've taken your advice by only focusing on the things I can control. Being clean and sober has given me a whole new lease on life. Psychologically, I'm meditating and practicing the breathing exercises. Whenever a negative situation arises, your voice magically appears in my head. Spiritually, my relationship with God has gotten a lot stronger. I realized that I was selfish for blaming Him and others for the nosedive of my life. Once I started accepting accountability, I understood that everything happens for a reason and it's usually for the greater good. Physically, I'm working out five days a week and have cut dairy, pork, and sugar completely from my diet.

Things between Eve and me have taken a one-eighty since I got incarcerated. She lifted the restraining order and she and the kids take the four-hour drive down once a month to visit, which I greatly appreciate. I even made amends with Gary. He's a good guy and I'm thankful that my children have a positive example of black love within their household. That's something I never experienced growing up and I'd be ignorant not to support them having it, regardless if I'm not the one currently able to provide it.

Trina and I are slowly working out our differences as well. We talk on the phone periodically and she often sends pics of Déjaun. I understand that I caused her a lot of damage. So, I'm being patient and gradually working towards regaining her trust. Hopefully, we'll be able to co-parent and put all the negativity behind us. One of my biggest regrets is the way I handled the paternity situation. Déjaun is such a wonderful little boy. He looks exactly the way I did at his age. I'm really looking forward to establishing a relationship with him once I get out.

A few months ago, I decided to take your advice by reaching out to Pops. Our connection was instant, and it reminded me of the old days. There wasn't even a need to ask about the things I'd been told as a child. We agreed that whatever bond we're building going forward, will be solely based on the present and the future. The knowledge and wisdom he's shared thus far is second to none, and for that, I'm extremely grateful. I'm excited to see what the future holds for us.

You'd be proud to know that I finally built up the courage to mail Momma the letter. To my surprise, she actually received it way better than I expected. In fact, she's had my back more than anyone through my "extended vacation." Momma has strongly been considering rehab and even agreed to join Tiffany and me in family counseling when I get out. That's the best news I've gotten since I've been in here. I don't know how long her epiphany will last, so I hope you leave some space open in your calendar.

My road to recovery is nowhere near finished. But, I'm proud to be able to say, I'm nowhere near where I used to be. And for that, I'll always have you to thank.

Sincerely,
Deshaun

THE END

All I Do Is Pen Publishing Presents

Whats Wrong With M.E.N.
By C.W. Burnett

Journey along as three, young, African-American ladies, from South Central Los Angeles, Monique Harris, Eve Nelson, and Na'Tosha Jimerson try to navigate through life, dealing with inconsistent partners and society's stigma of being angry, black women. When it comes to being let down by their significant other, the million-dollar question remains: are men the ones truly at fault? Or, is it actually the "M.E.N." from within who're to blame?

www.allidoispen.com
Instagram: all_i_do_is_pen • Facebook: C.W. Burnett

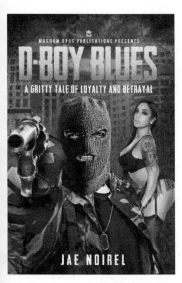

Magnum Opus Publications Presents

D-Boy Blues:
A Gritty Tale of Loyalty and Betrayal
By Jae Noirel

Blue and Bobby grew up together as best friends. Blue is a street smart Hustler being raised in foster care and Bobby is a scrawny nerd who lives with his sister and abusive father. As kids, Blue protects Bobby from neighborhood bullies but as they grow older they grow apart. Bobby grows up to be an Oakland police officer and Blue becomes a prominent drug dealer. This unlikely pair are put at odds once they cross paths in the street and both love and loyalties will be tested. D-Boy Blues is a classic story of love, betrayal, redemption and police corruption.

www.MagnumOpusPublications.com
Instagram: mgnm_opus • Facebook: Magnum Opus Publications

Made in the USA
Middletown, DE
06 July 2024

56961758R00087